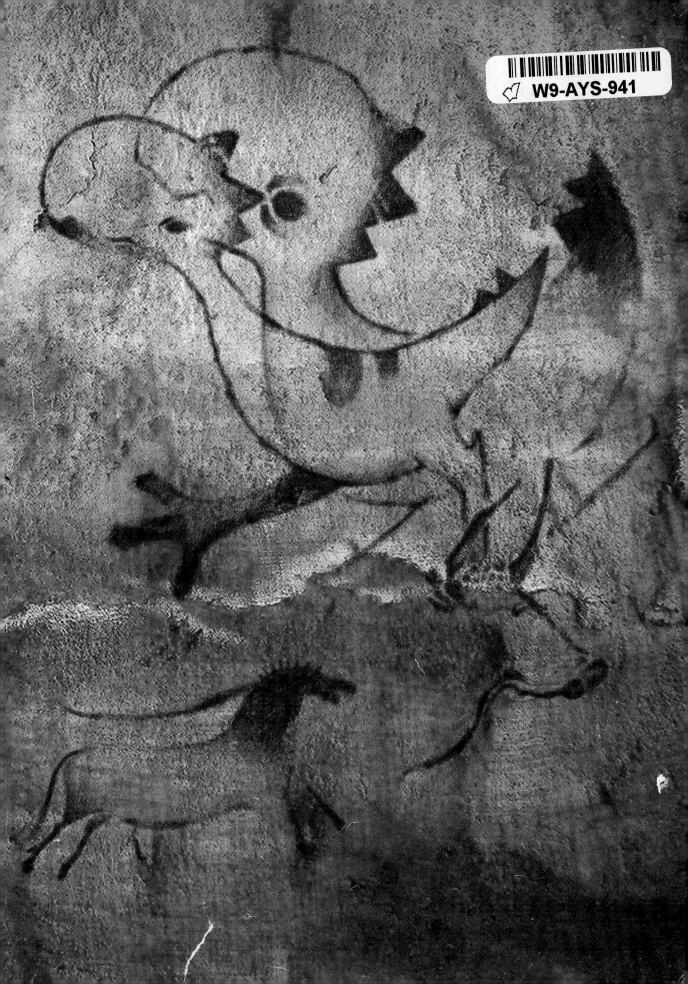

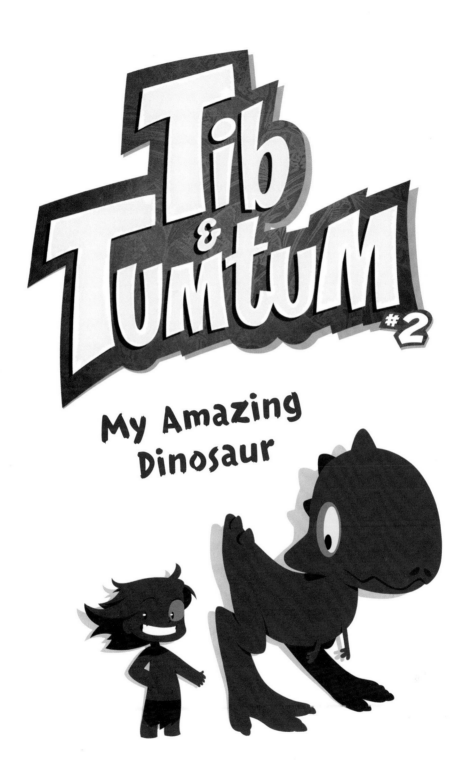

Tib & Tumtum #2

My Amazing Dinosaur

story
Grimaldi

art
Bannister

colors
Grimaldi

Graphic Universe™ • Minneapolis

For Papa.
Thank you to all my friends--girls, boys, cats, chickens, hairy, feathered,
scaly, winged. I love you all very much.
--Grimaldi

Thanks to Jean-Claude, Anne, Eric, and Carol.
And of course, thanks to Flora, for all that there is in this book and author.
--Bannister

Story by Grimaldi
Art by Bannister
Coloring by Grimaldi

Translation by Carol Klio Burrell

First American edition published in 2014 by Graphic Universe™.

Mon dinosaure a du talent by Grimaldi & Bannister © 2013—Glénat Editions
Copyright © 2014 by Lerner Publishing Group, Inc., for the US edition

Graphic Universe™ is a trademark of Lerner Publishing Group, Inc.

Graphic Universe™
A division of Lerner Publishing Group, Inc.
241 First Avenue North
Minneapolis, MN 55401 USA

For reading levels and more information, look up this title at www.lernerbooks.com.

Library of Congress Cataloging-in-Publication Data

Grimaldi, 1975–
     [Mon dinosaure a du talent! English]
     My amazing dinosaur / by Grimaldi ; illustrated by Bannister ; translation by Carol Klio Burrell. — First
American edition.
          p.   cm. — (Tib & Tumtum ; #2)
     Summary: Tib and his dinosaur friend Tumtum are back for more prehistoric (mis)adventures in the
second installment of the Tib & Tumtum series.
     ISBN 978-1-4677-1298-9 (lib. bdg. : alk. paper)
     ISBN 978-1-4677-2427-2 (eBook)
     1. Graphic novels. [1. Graphic novels. 2. Prehistoric peoples—Fiction. 3. Dinosaurs—Fiction.]
     I. Bannister, illustrator. II. Burrell, Carol Klio, translator. III. Title.
PZ7.7.6758My 2014
741.5'315—dc23   2013036088

Manufactured in the United States of America
1 – BP – 12/31/2013

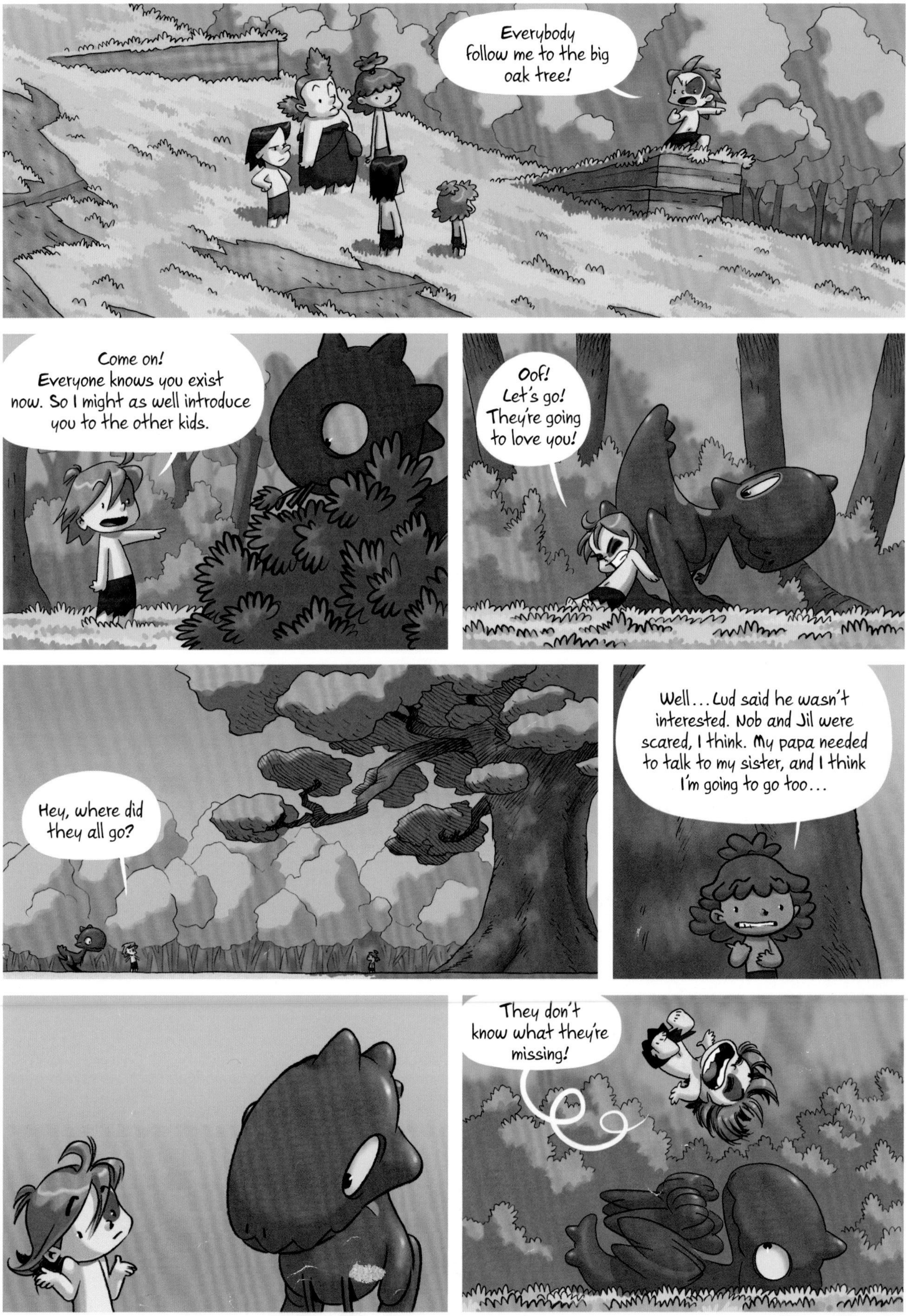
Everybody follow me to the big oak tree!
Come on! Everyone knows you exist now. So I might as well introduce you to the other kids.
Oof! Let's go! They're going to love you!
Hey, where did they all go?
Well... Lud said he wasn't interested. Nob and Jil were scared, I think. My papa needed to talk to my sister, and I think I'm going to go too...
They don't know what they're missing!

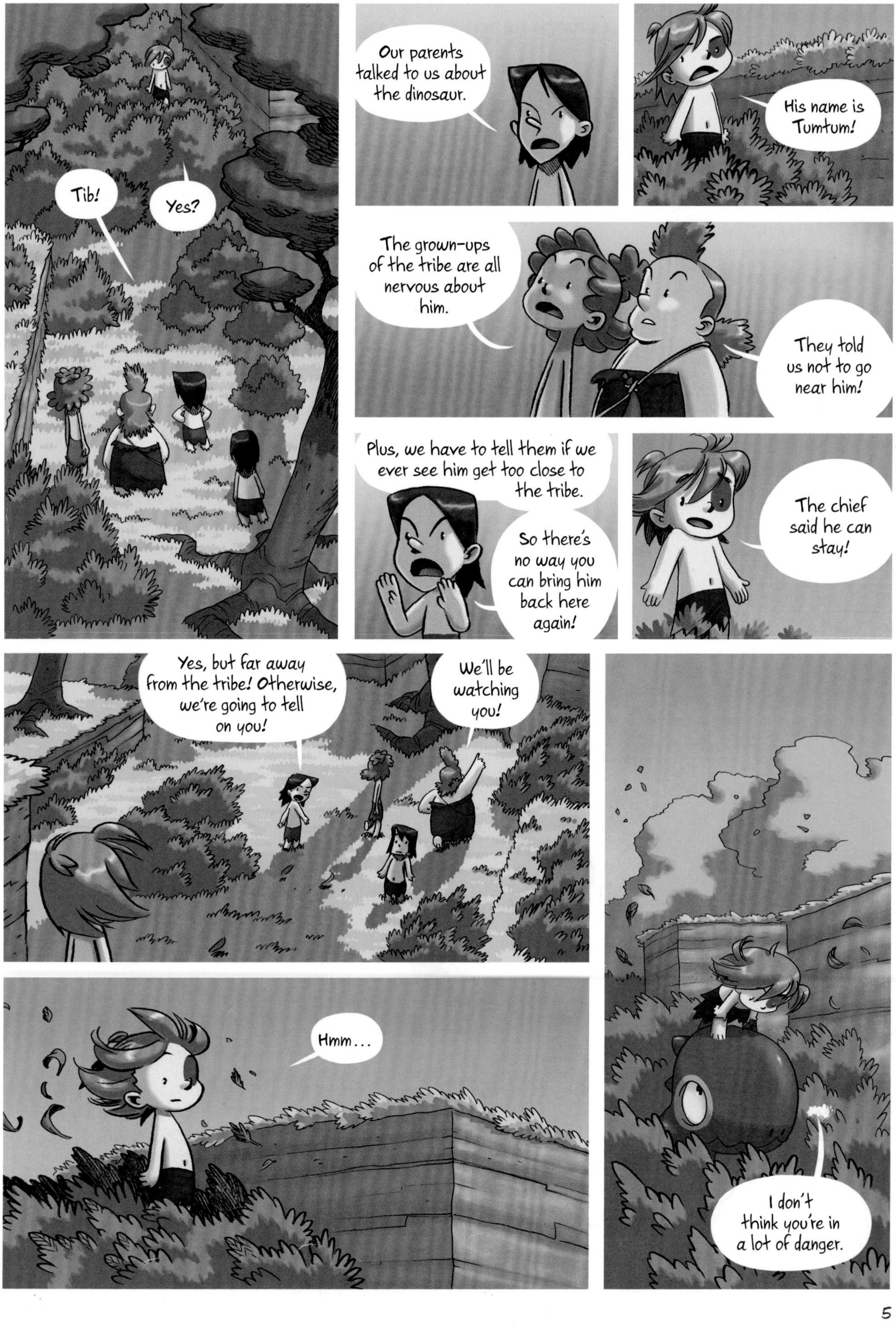

Tib!
Yes?
Our parents talked to us about the dinosaur.
His name is Tumtum!
The grown-ups of the tribe are all nervous about him.
They told us not to go near him!
Plus, we have to tell them if we ever see him get too close to the tribe.
So there's no way you can bring him back here again!
The chief said he can stay!
Yes, but far away from the tribe! Otherwise, we're going to tell on you!
We'll be watching you!
Hmm...
I don't think you're in a lot of danger.

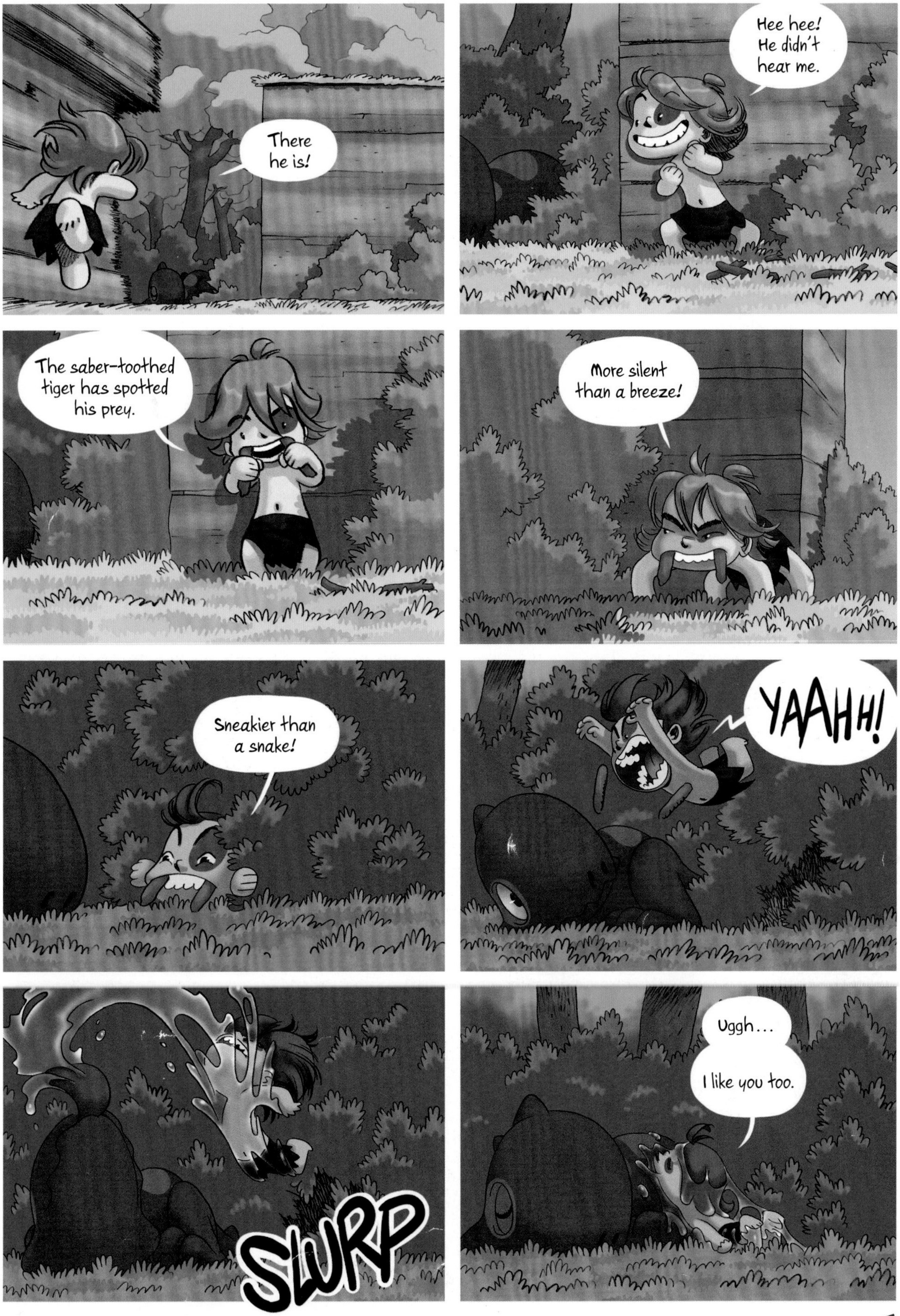
There he is!
Hee hee! He didn't hear me.
The saber-toothed tiger has spotted his prey.
More silent than a breeze!
Sneakier than a snake!
YAAHH!
SLURP
Uggh...
I like you too.

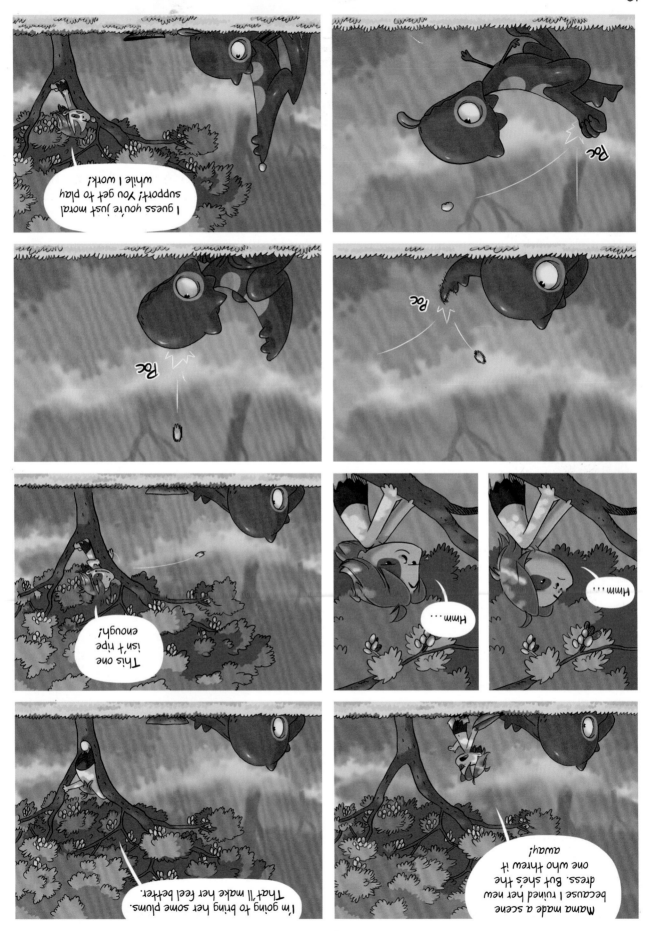

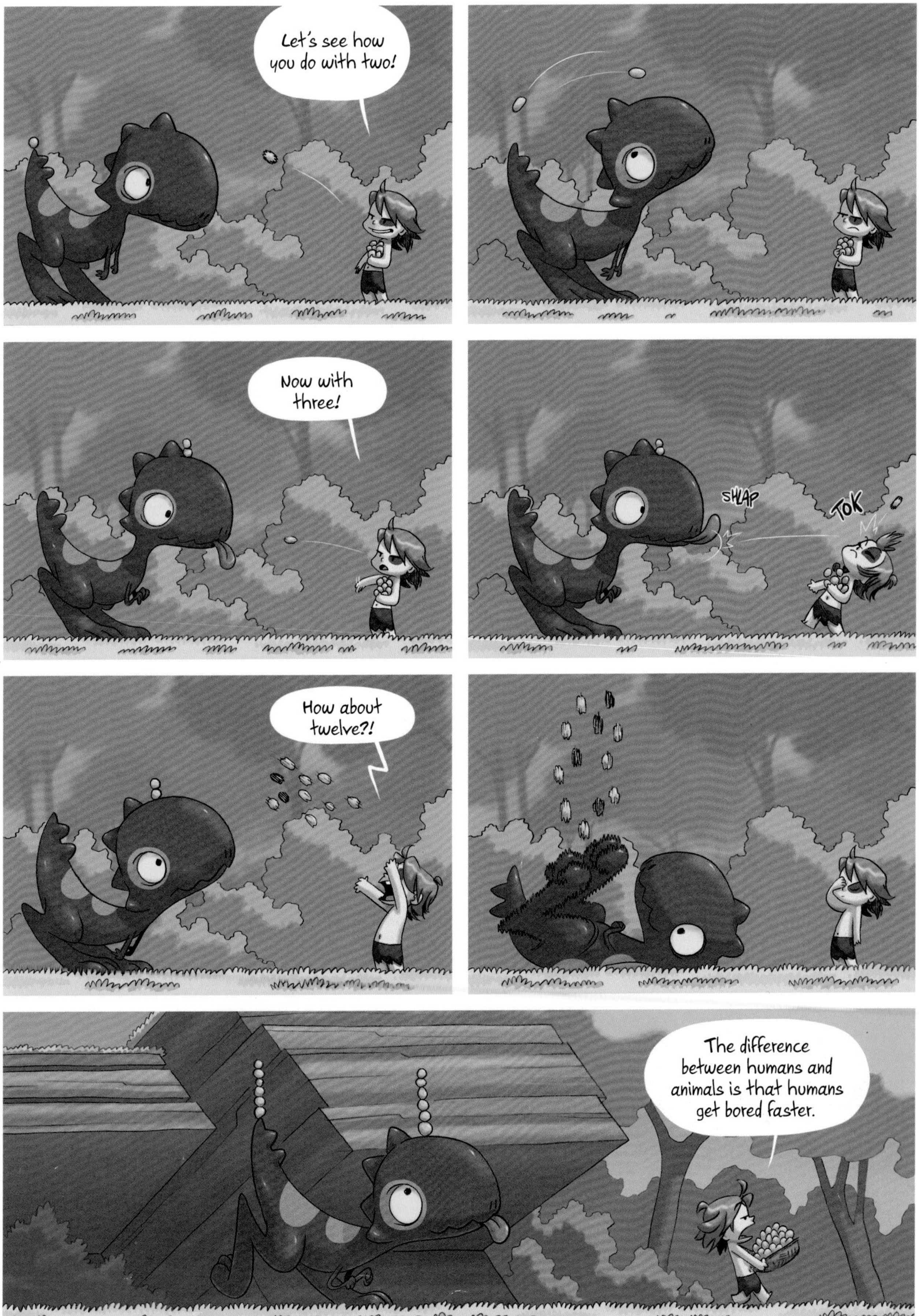

Let's see how you do with two!
Now with three!
SHLAP
TOK
How about twelve?!
The difference between humans and animals is that humans get bored faster.

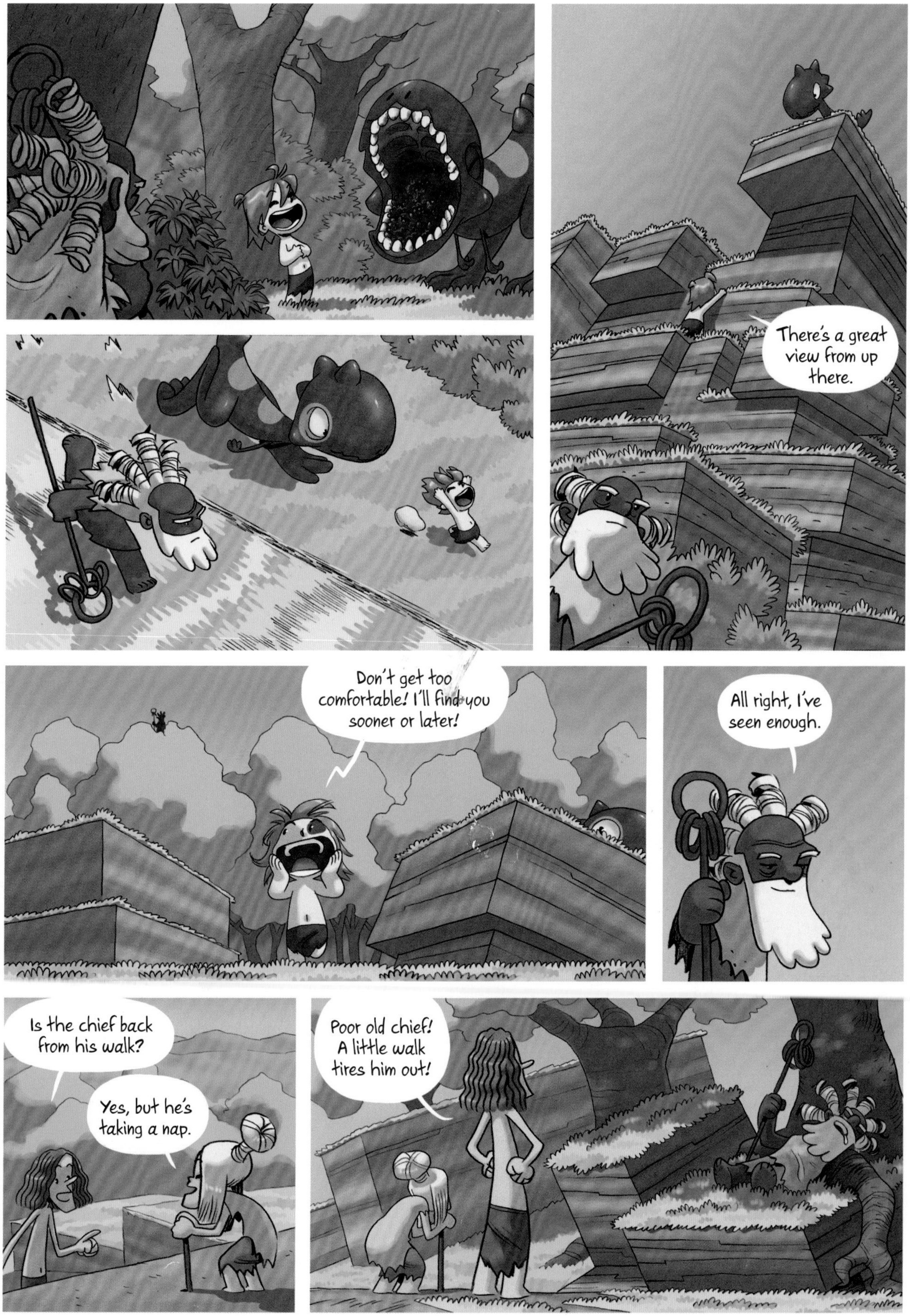
There's a great view from up there.
Don't get too comfortable! I'll find you sooner or later!
All right, I've seen enough.
Is the chief back from his walk?
Yes, but he's taking a nap.
Poor old chief! A little walk tires him out!

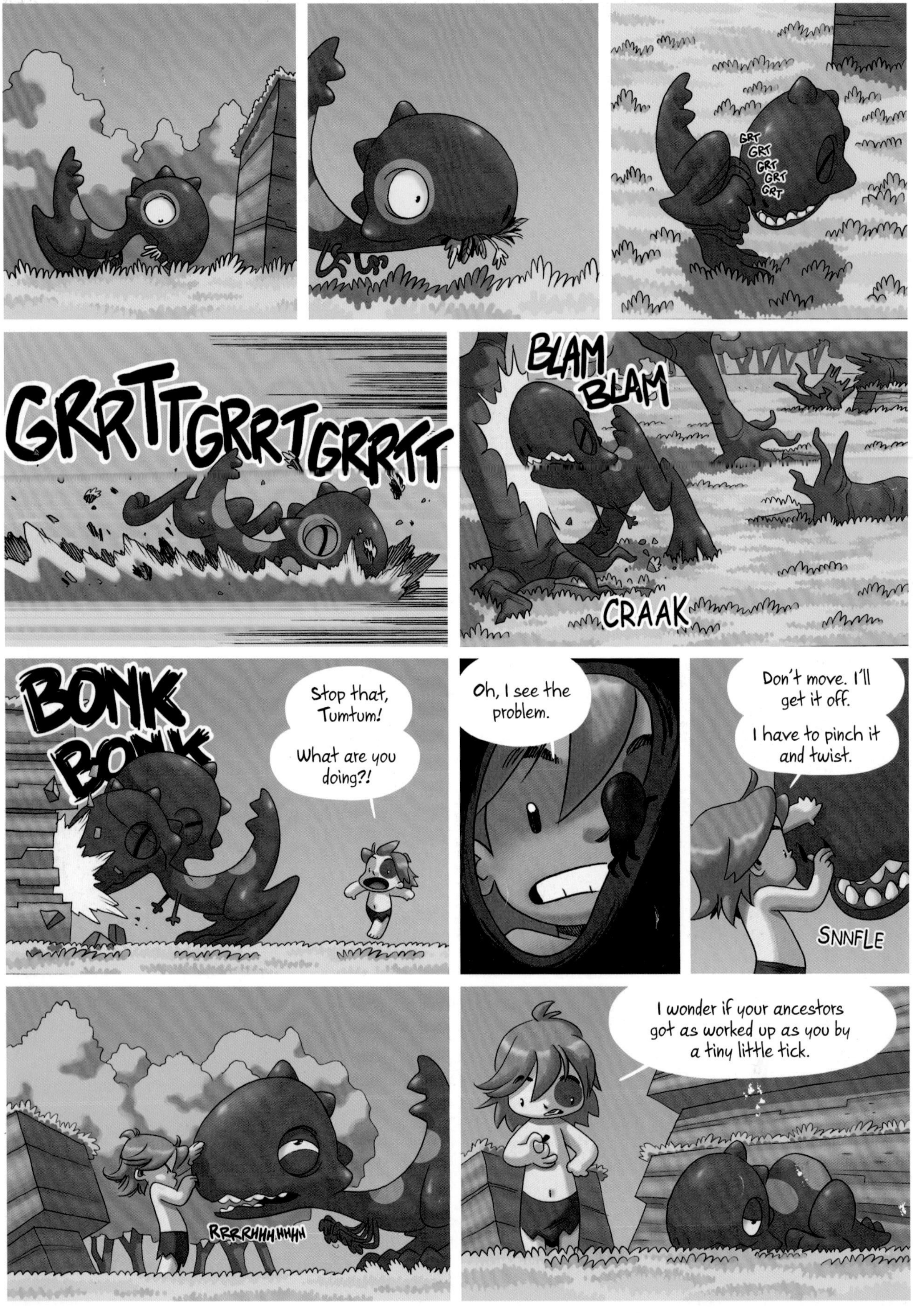
GRT GRT GRT GRT GRT
GRRTTGRRTGRRTT
BLAM BLAM
CRAAK
BONK BONK
Stop that, Tumtum!
What are you doing?!
Oh, I see the problem.
Don't move. I'll get it off.
I have to pinch it and twist.
SNNFLE
RRRRHHH HHHH
I wonder if your ancestors got as worked up as you by a tiny little tick.

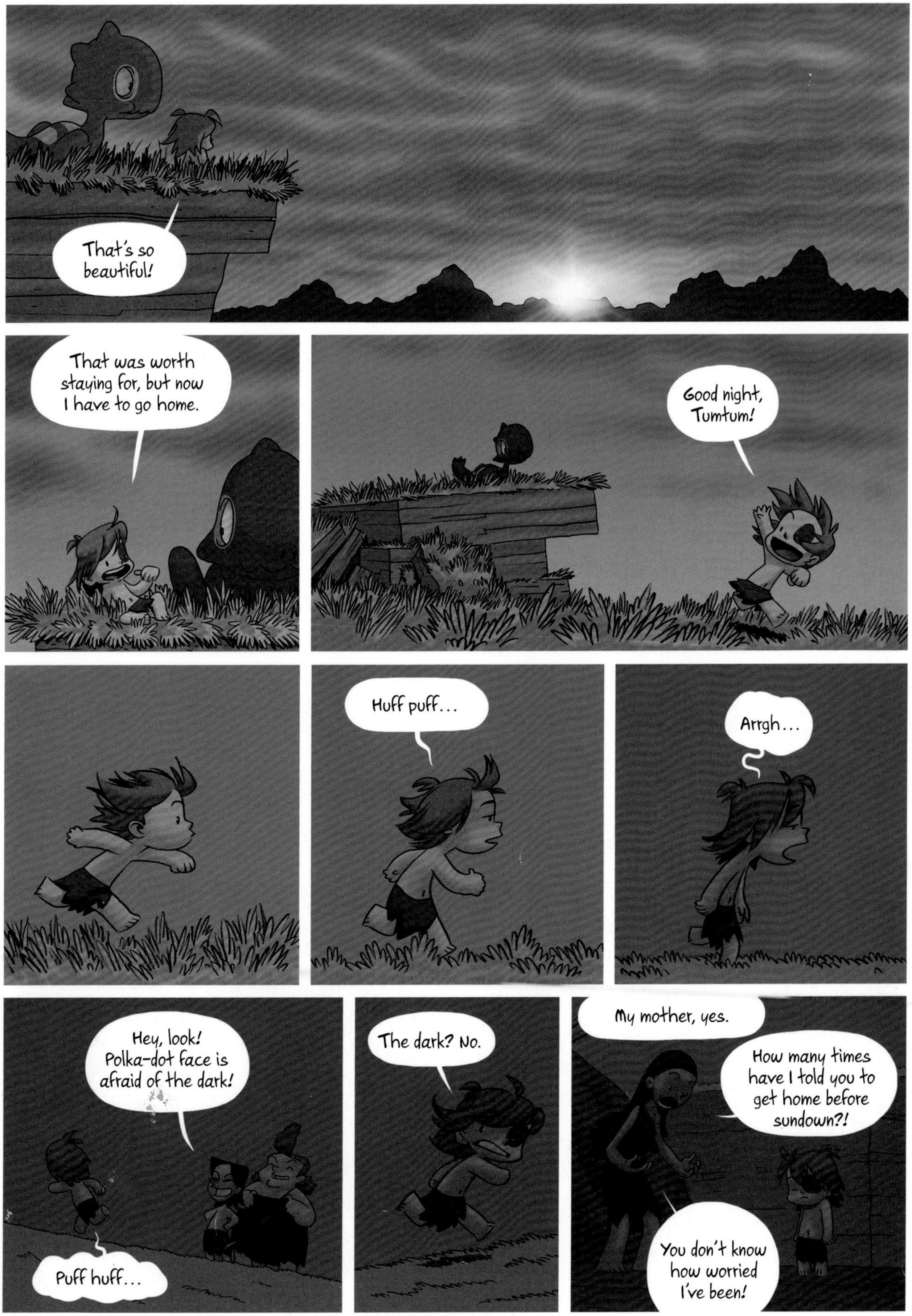
That's so beautiful!
That was worth staying for, but now I have to go home.
Good night, Tumtum!
Huff puff...
Arrgh...
Hey, look! Polka-dot face is afraid of the dark!
Puff huff...
The dark? No.
My mother, yes.
How many times have I told you to get home before sundown?!
You don't know how worried I've been!

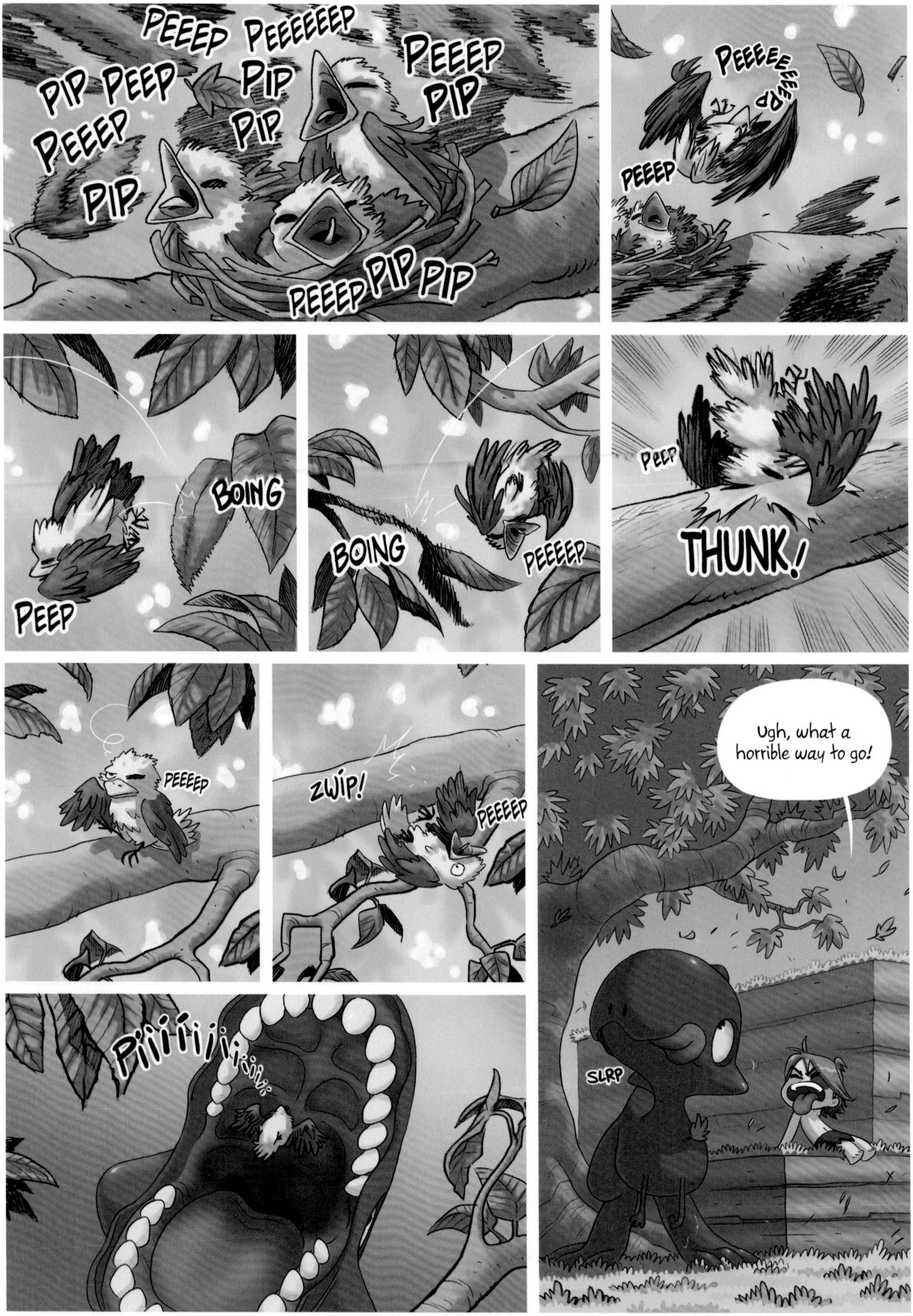
PEEEP PEEEEEEP
PIP PEEP
PEEEP
PIP
PIP
PIP
PEEEP
PIP
PEEEP PIP PIP
PEEEEEEEEP
PEEEP
PEEP
BOING
BOING
PEEEEP
PEEP
THUNK!
PEEEEP
ZWIP!
PEEEEP
Piiiiiiiiiii
Ugh, what a horrible way to go!
SLRP

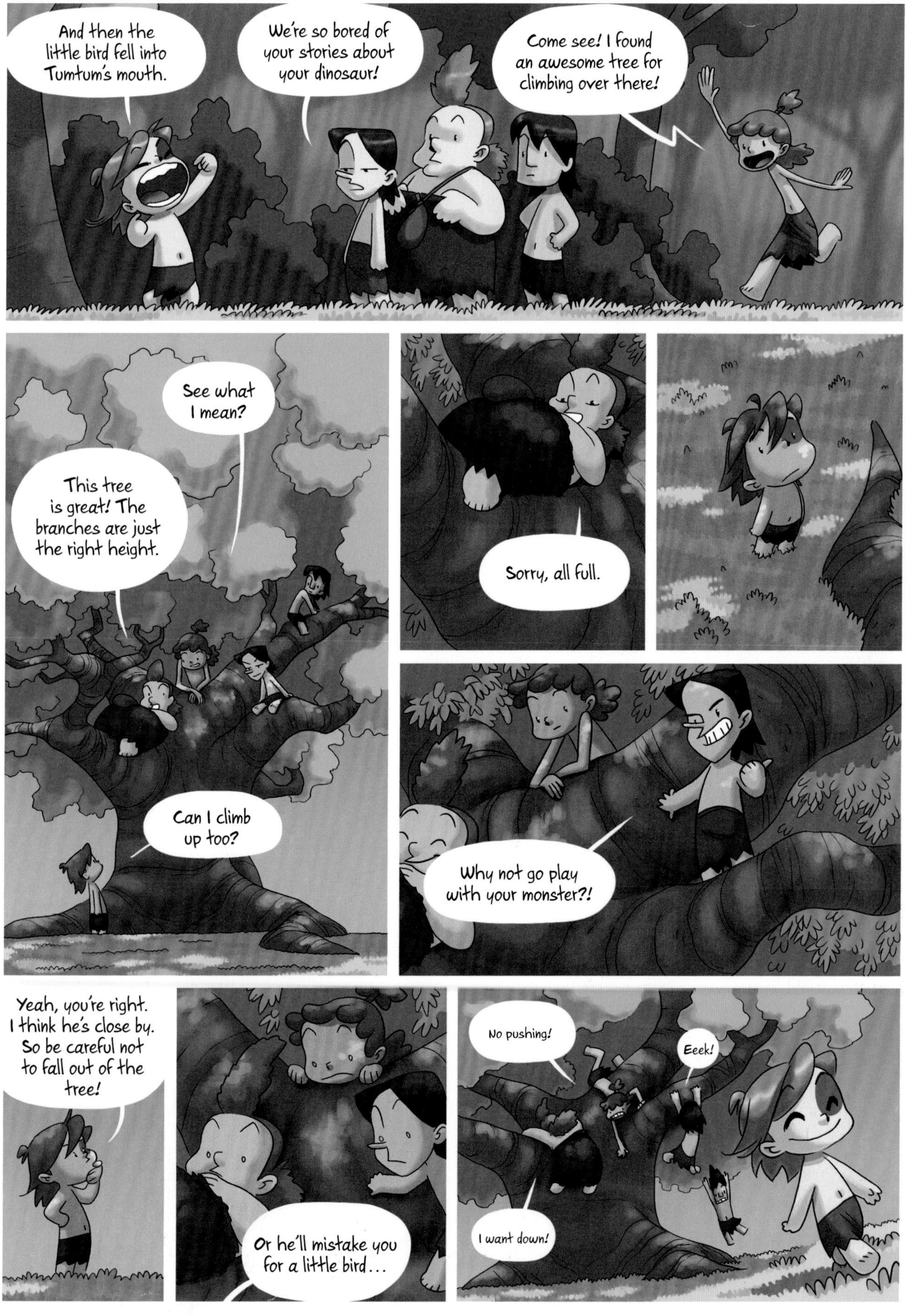
And then the little bird fell into Tumtum's mouth.
We're so bored of your stories about your dinosaur!
Come see! I found an awesome tree for climbing over there!
See what I mean?
This tree is great! The branches are just the right height.
Can I climb up too?
Sorry, all full.
Why not go play with your monster?!
Yeah, you're right. I think he's close by. So be careful not to fall out of the tree!
Or he'll mistake you for a little bird...
No pushing!
Eeek!
I want down!

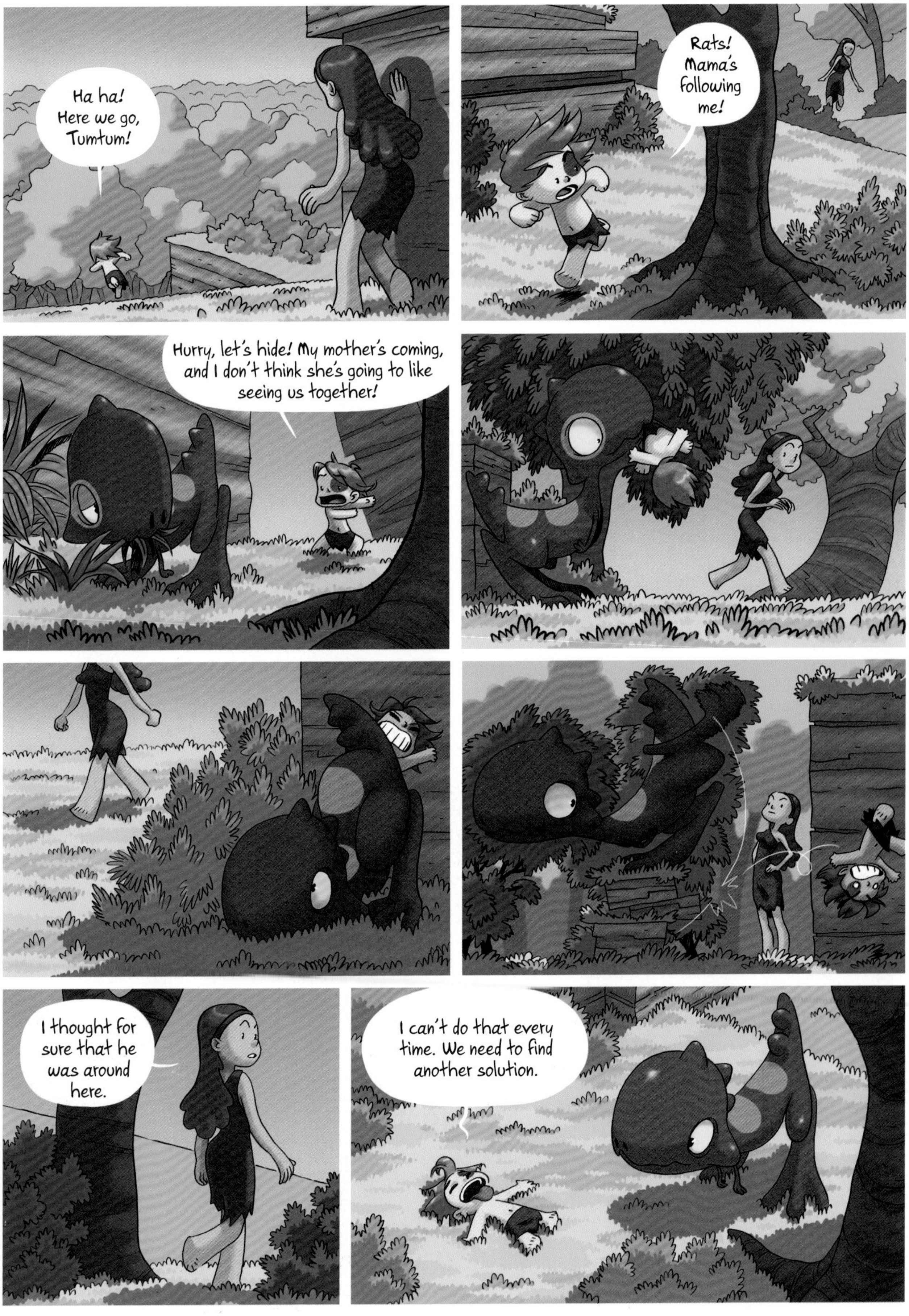

Ha ha! Here we go, Tumtum!
Rats! Mama's following me!
Hurry, let's hide! My mother's coming, and I don't think she's going to like seeing us together!
I thought for sure that he was around here.
I can't do that every time. We need to find another solution.

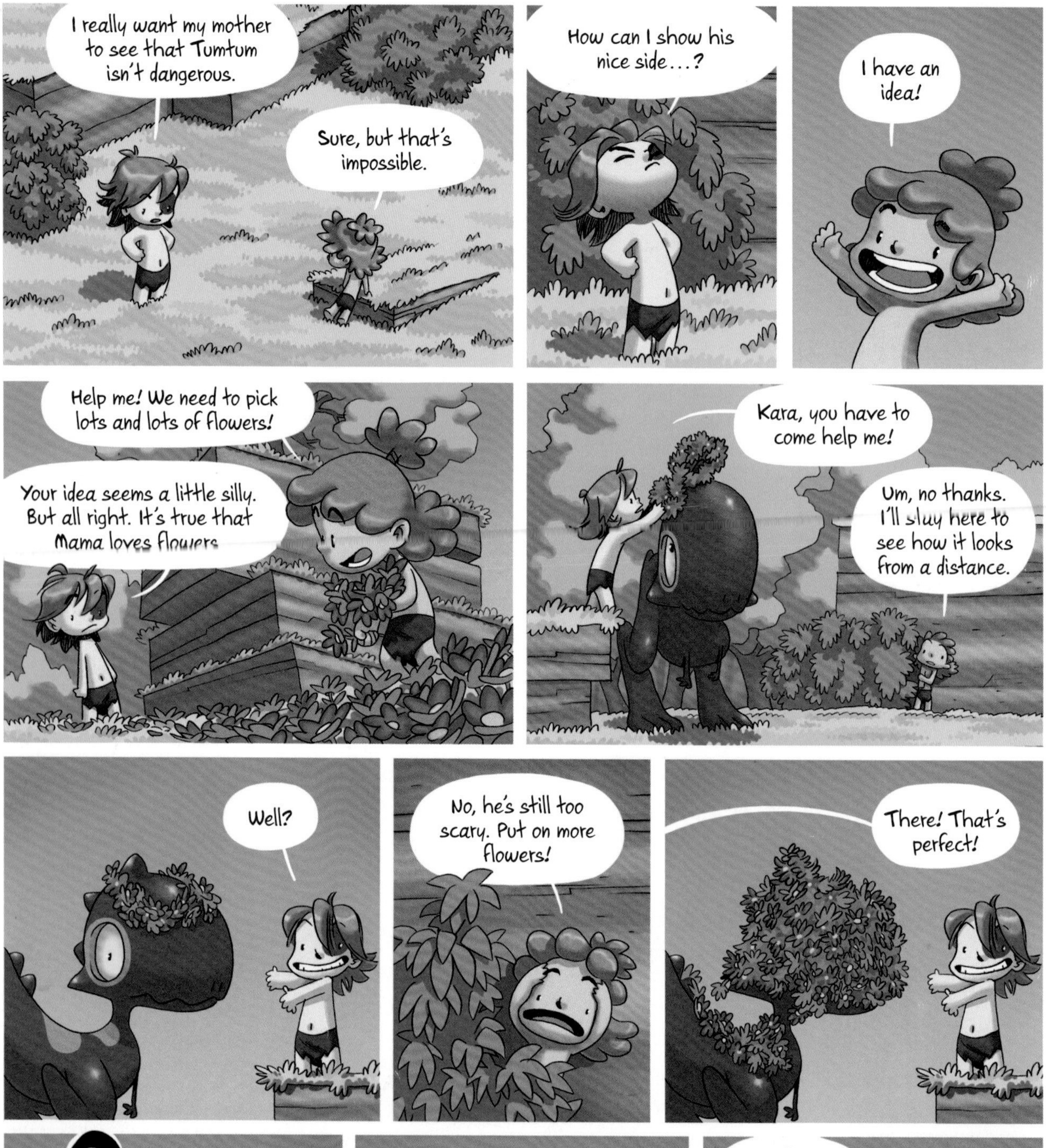
I really want my mother to see that Tumtum isn't dangerous.
Sure, but that's impossible.
How can I show his nice side...?
I have an idea!
Help me! We need to pick lots and lots of flowers!
Your idea seems a little silly. But all right. It's true that Mama loves flowers
Kara, you have to come help me!
Um, no thanks. I'll stay here to see how it looks from a distance.
Well?
No, he's still too scary. Put on more flowers!
There! That's perfect!
SLURP
MUNCH
MUNCH
WAAAAAAHH! All those pretty flowers!
Aw, stop crying! That was a pretty bad idea, anyway.

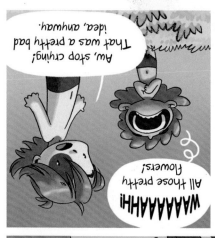

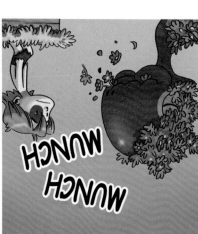

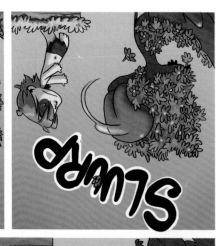

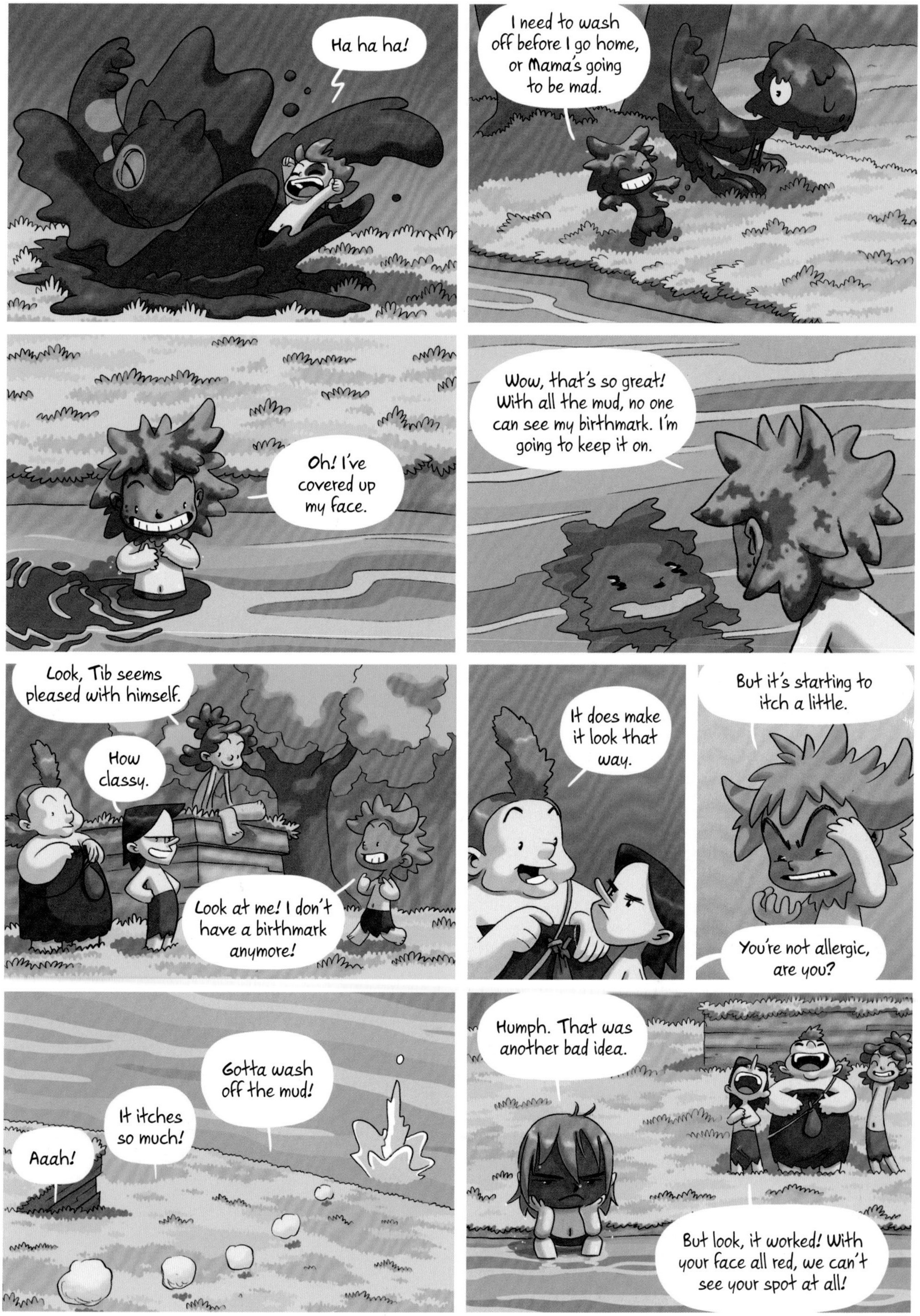
Ha ha ha!
I need to wash off before I go home, or Mama's going to be mad.
Oh! I've covered up my face.
Wow, that's so great! With all the mud, no one can see my birthmark. I'm going to keep it on.
Look, Tib seems pleased with himself.
How classy.
Look at me! I don't have a birthmark anymore!
It does make it look that way.
But it's starting to itch a little.
You're not allergic, are you?
Aaah!
It itches so much!
Gotta wash off the mud!
Humph. That was another bad idea.
But look, it worked! With your face all red, we can't see your spot at all!

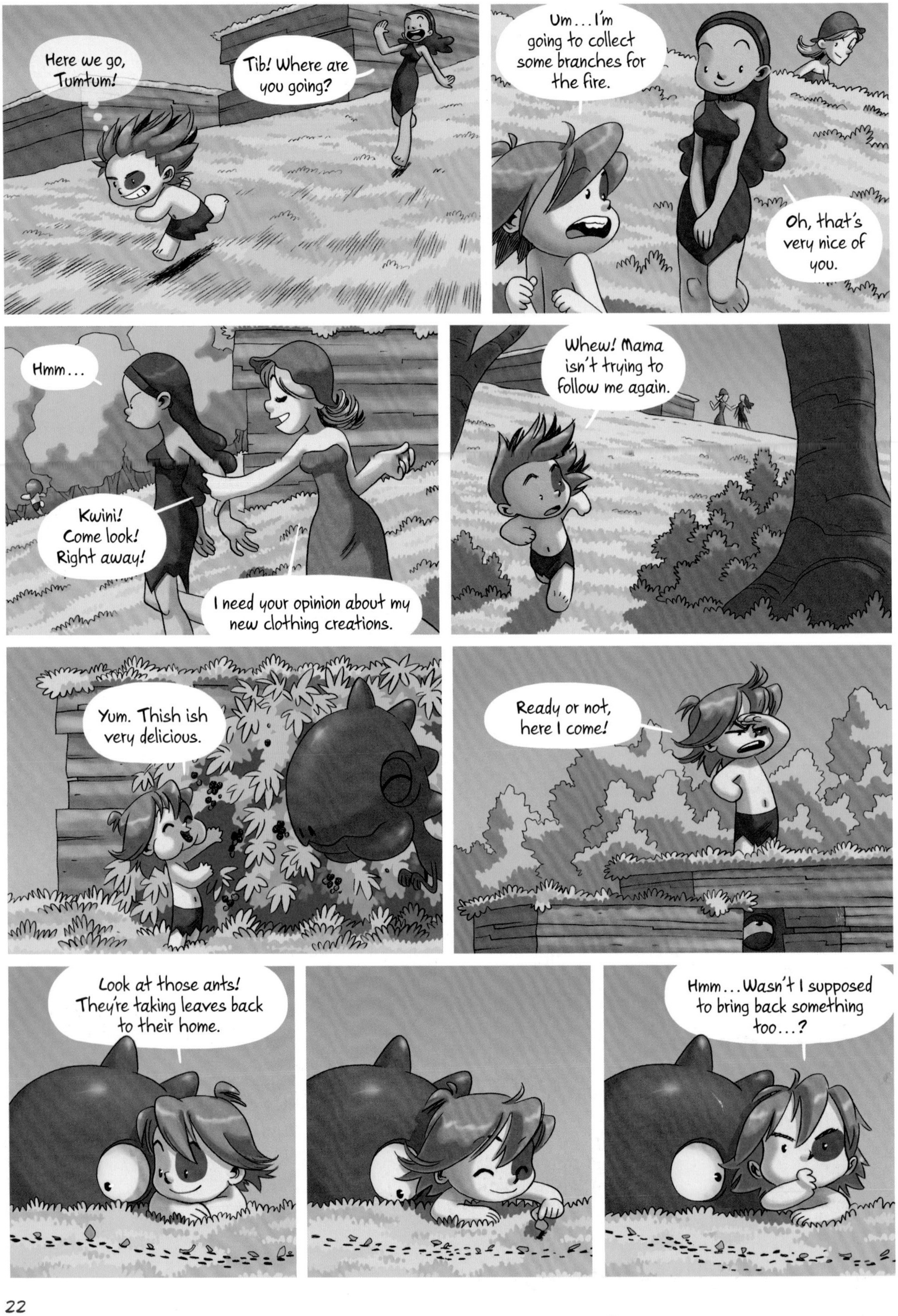
Here we go, Tumtum!
Tib! Where are you going?
Um...I'm going to collect some branches for the fire.
Oh, that's very nice of you.
Hmm...
Kwini! Come look! Right away!
I need your opinion about my new clothing creations.
Whew! Mama isn't trying to follow me again.
Yum. Thish ish very delicious.
Ready or not, here I come!
Look at those ants! They're taking leaves back to their home.
Hmm...Wasn't I supposed to bring back something too...?

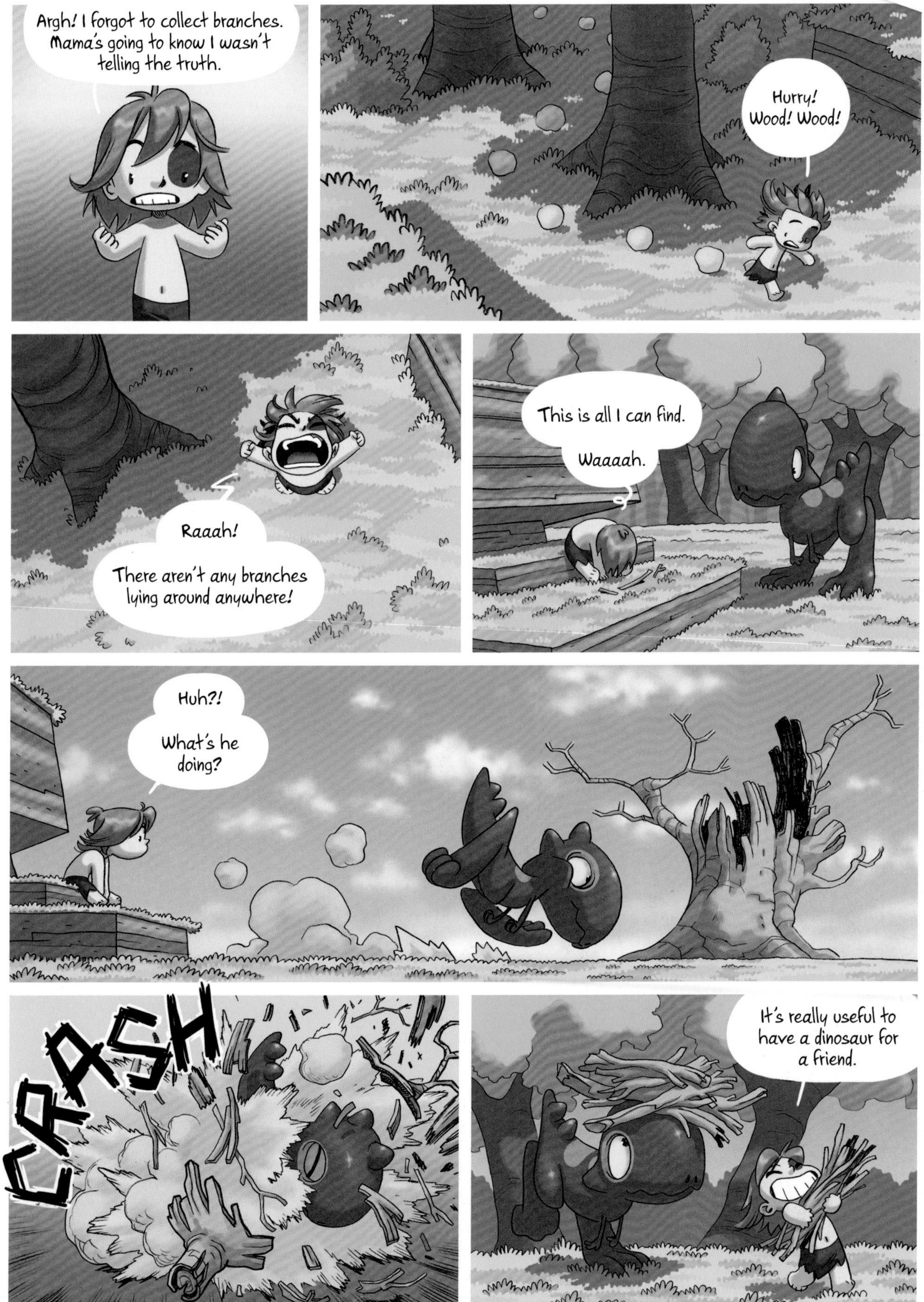
Argh! I forgot to collect branches. Mama's going to know I wasn't telling the truth.
Hurry! Wood! Wood!
Raaah!
There aren't any branches lying around anywhere!
This is all I can find.
Waaaah.
Huh?!
What's he doing?
CRASH
It's really useful to have a dinosaur for a friend.

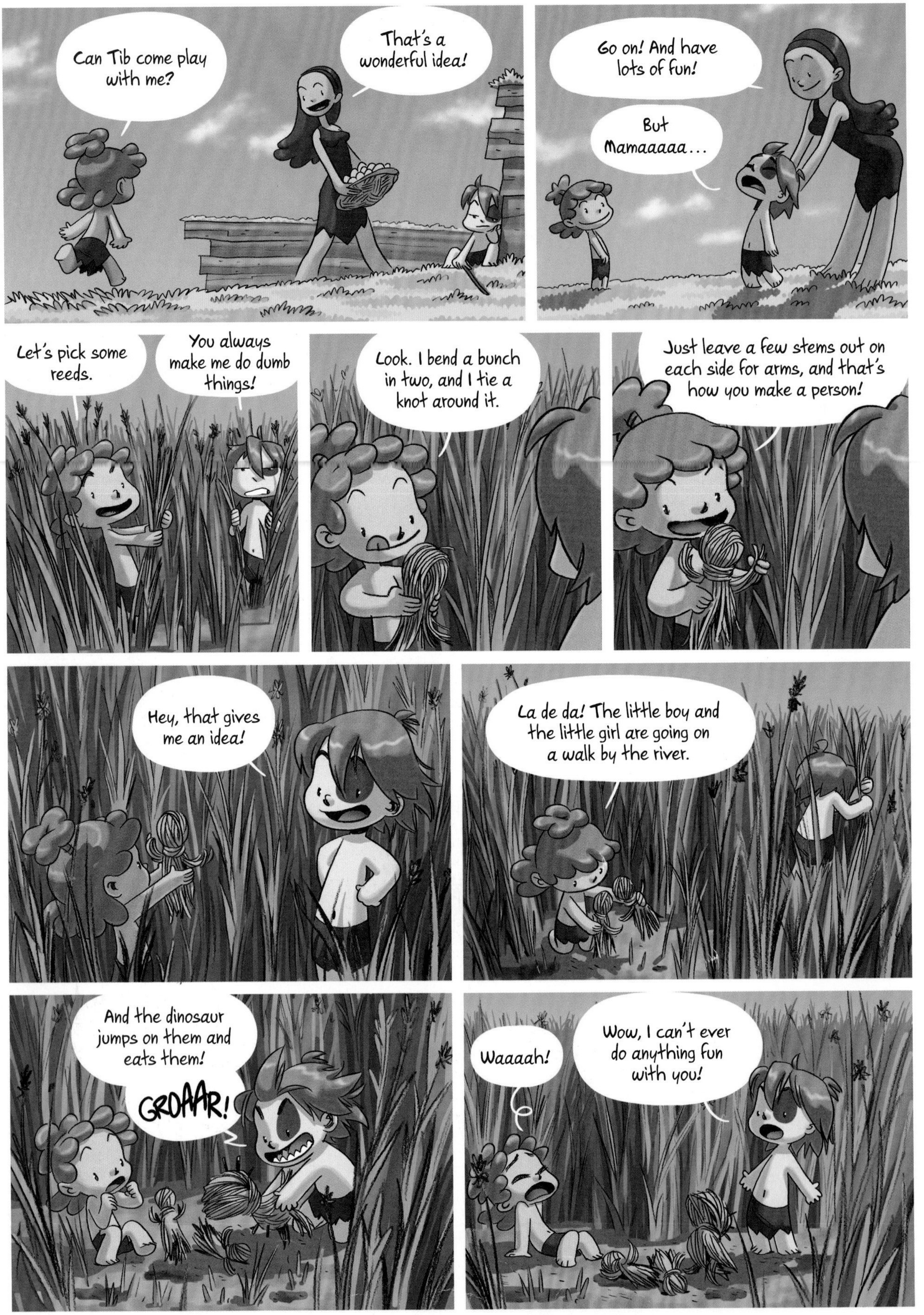
Can Tib come play with me?
That's a wonderful idea!
Go on! And have lots of fun!
But Mamaaaaa...
Let's pick some reeds.
You always make me do dumb things!
Look. I bend a bunch in two, and I tie a knot around it.
Just leave a few stems out on each side for arms, and that's how you make a person!
Hey, that gives me an idea!
La de da! The little boy and the little girl are going on a walk by the river.
And the dinosaur jumps on them and eats them!
GROAAR!
Waaaah!
Wow, I can't ever do anything fun with you!

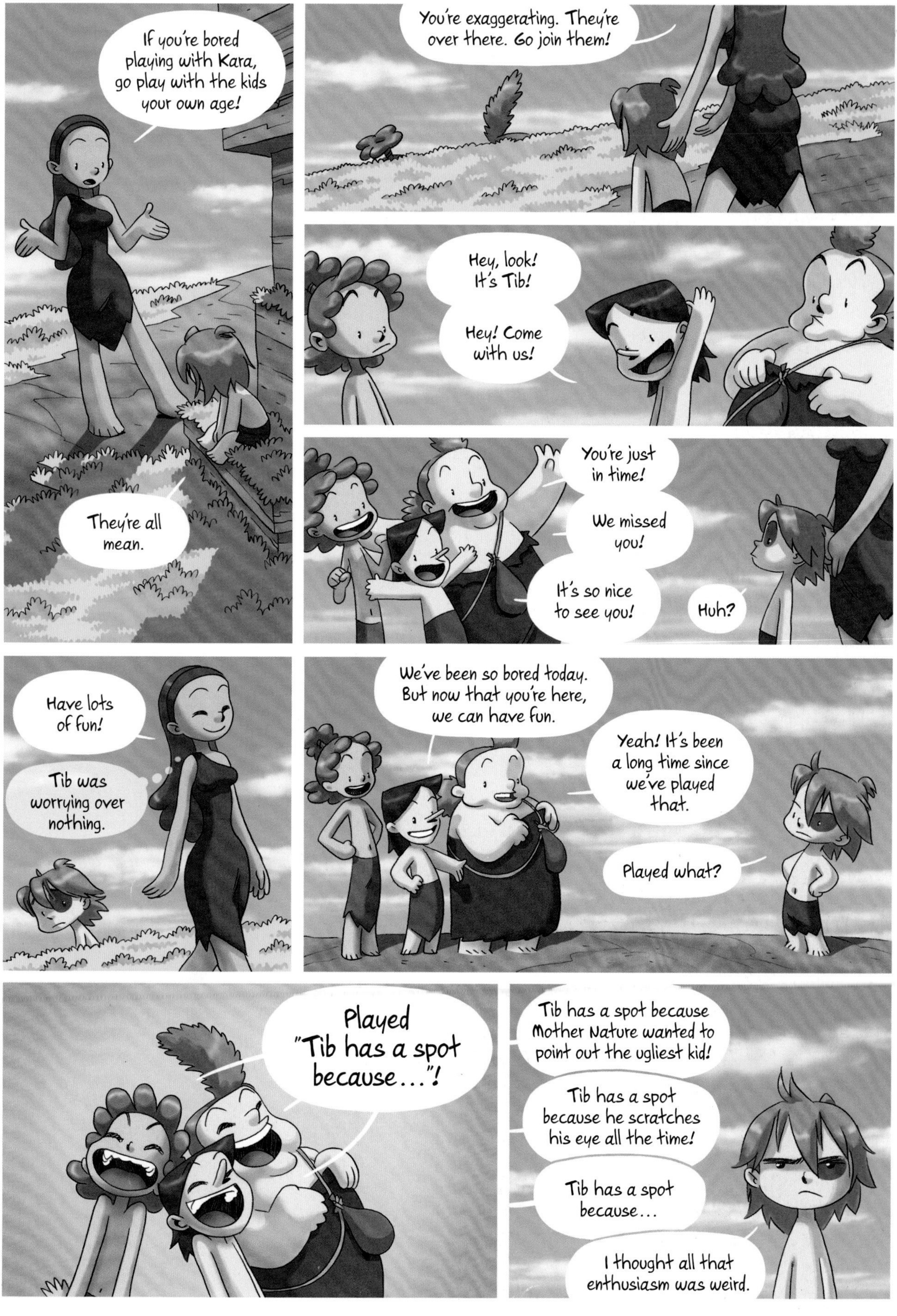
If you're bored playing with Kara, go play with the kids your own age!
They're all mean.
You're exaggerating. They're over there. Go join them!
Hey, look! It's Tib!
Hey! Come with us!
You're just in time!
We missed you!
It's so nice to see you!
Huh?
Have lots of fun!
Tib was worrying over nothing.
We've been so bored today. But now that you're here, we can have fun.
Yeah! It's been a long time since we've played that.
Played what?
Played "Tib has a spot because..."!
Tib has a spot because Mother Nature wanted to point out the ugliest kid!
Tib has a spot because he scratches his eye all the time!
Tib has a spot because...
I thought all that enthusiasm was weird.

You again?

Uh...can I play with you, maybe?

Sure. If you want to play "Tib has a spot because" again.

Um, no!

Then go away!

We don't need you here.

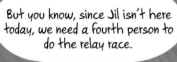

But you know, since Jil isn't here today, we need a fourth person to do the relay race.

Are you kidding? He's too clumsy!

Yeah, why don't you go play with your monster?

Tumtum isn't a monster! In fact, I'd rather go be with him!

But my mother would rather I play with you.

Aha! You see? He doesn't want to join us at all! His mother is making him!

Aw, come on! Be nice!

We can try, just for today.

I don't care. You two do what you want.

But but but...if we let Tib into our gang, we won't be cool anymore!

And after that, anything could happen!

Oh, Tib's here! Can I play with you?

That's it! That's what I mean.

29

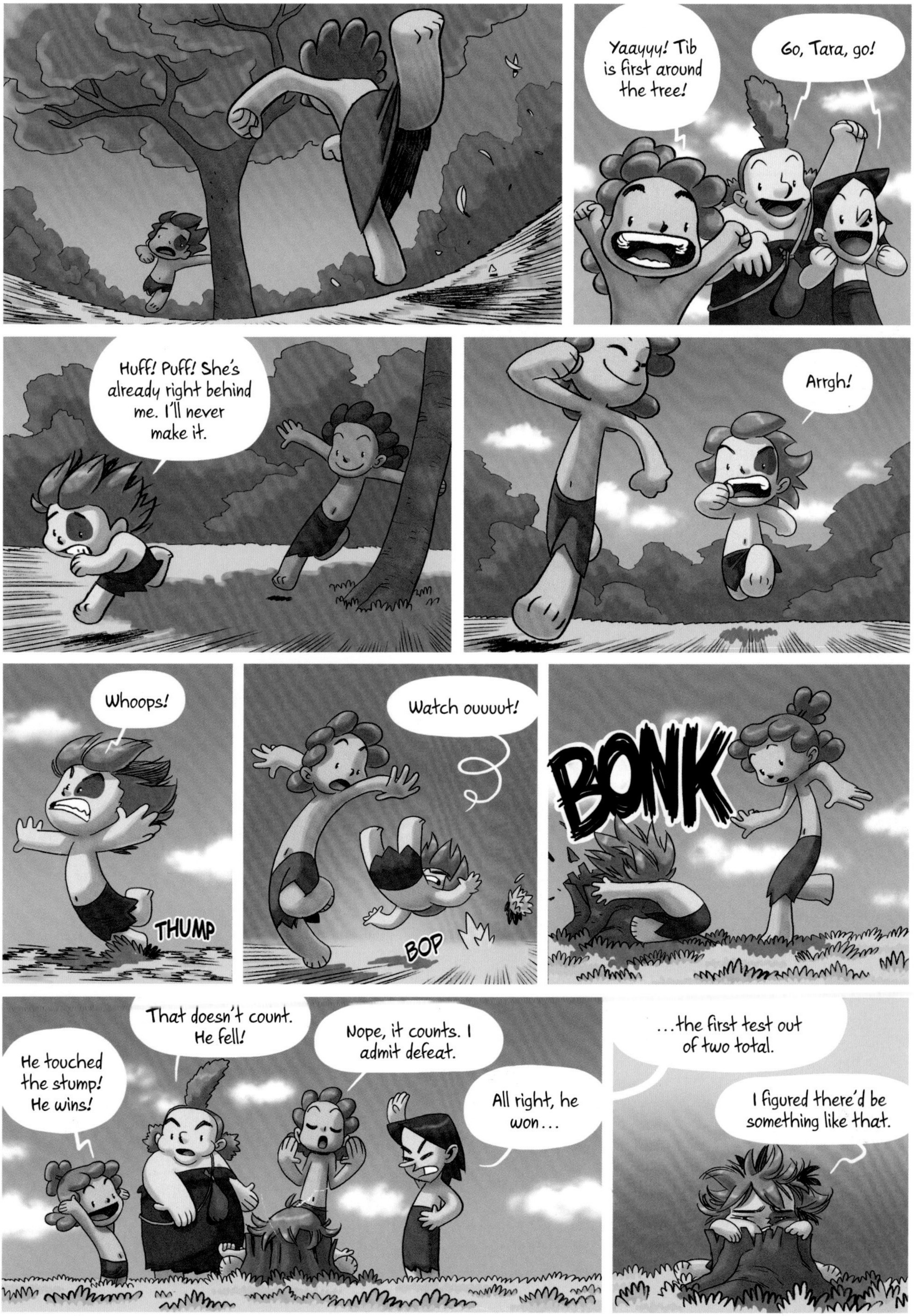

Yaayyy! Tib is first around the tree!
Go, Tara, go!
Huff! Puff! She's already right behind me. I'll never make it.
Arrgh!
Whoops!
THUMP
Watch ouuuut!
BOP
BONK
He touched the stump! He wins!
That doesn't count. He fell!
Nope, it counts. I admit defeat.
All right, he won...
...the first test out of two total.
I figured there'd be something like that.

Be very careful.

Always try to keep three points of support.

The things I do to make my mother happy!

I'm not scared!

I can do it!

Looks like the easiest thing is for you to give up now, if you're scared.

You're completely crazy! I'm going to tell his parents!

Come back here, tattletale!

Don't be silly! He'll never get that high.

If he falls off, he'll break all his bones.

He'll give up before that, and we'll be rid of him.

She's right. I've never even gotten past where the rock hangs over.

It's way too dangerous! Are you trying to get Tib hurt?!

What?! But that's impossible!

For the second test, you have to climb all the way up that cliff.

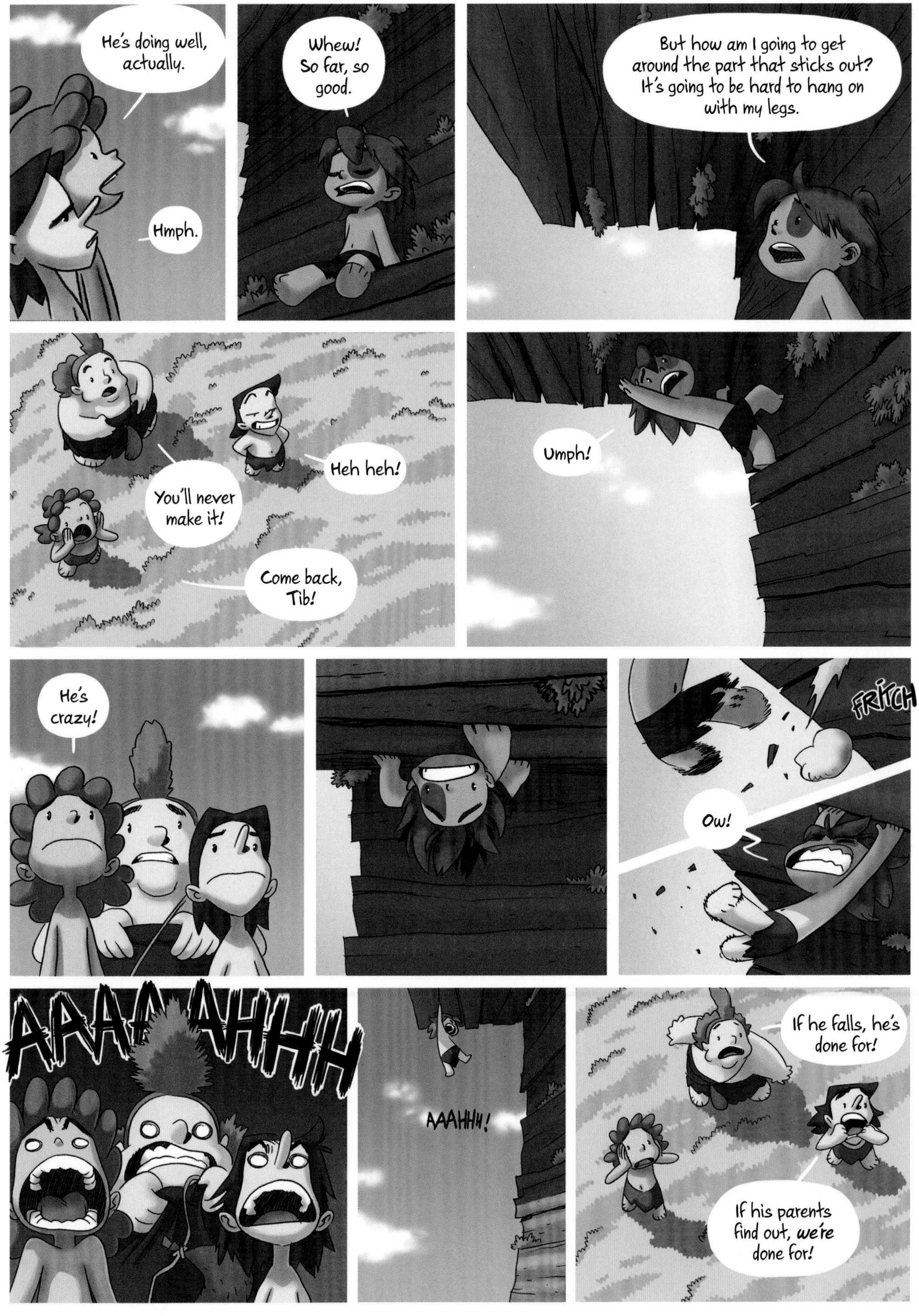
He's doing well, actually.
Hmph.
Whew! So far, so good.
But how am I going to get around the part that sticks out? It's going to be hard to hang on with my legs.
You'll never make it!
Heh heh!
Come back, Tib!
Umph!
He's crazy!
FRITCH
Ow!
AAAAAHHH
AAAHHH!
If he falls, he's done for!
If his parents find out, we're done for!

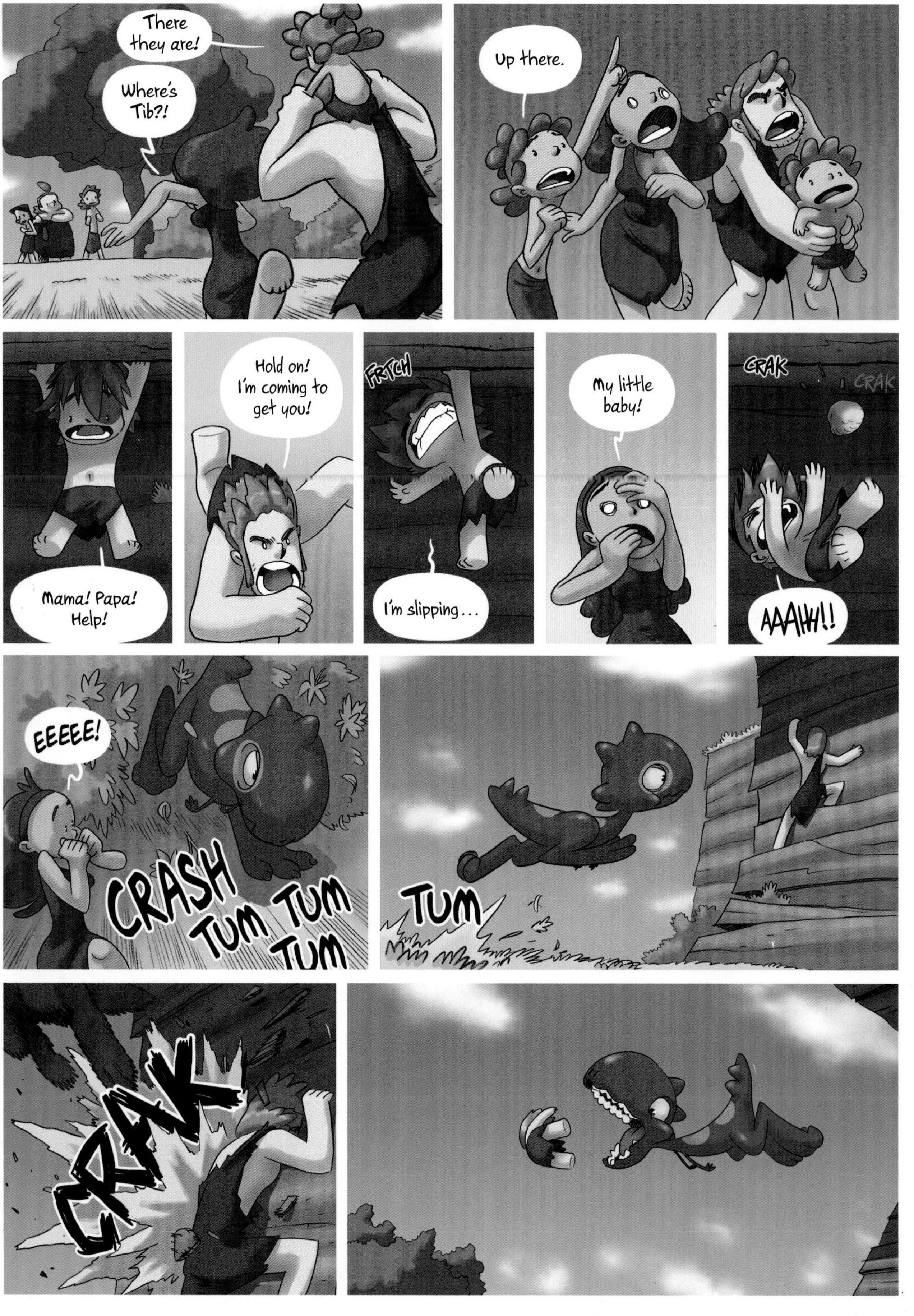
There they are!
Where's Tib?!
Up there.
Mama! Papa! Help!
Hold on! I'm coming to get you!
FRTCH
I'm slipping...
My little baby!
CRAK
CRAK
AAAHH!!
EEEEE!
CRASH
TUM TUM
TUM
TUM
CRAK

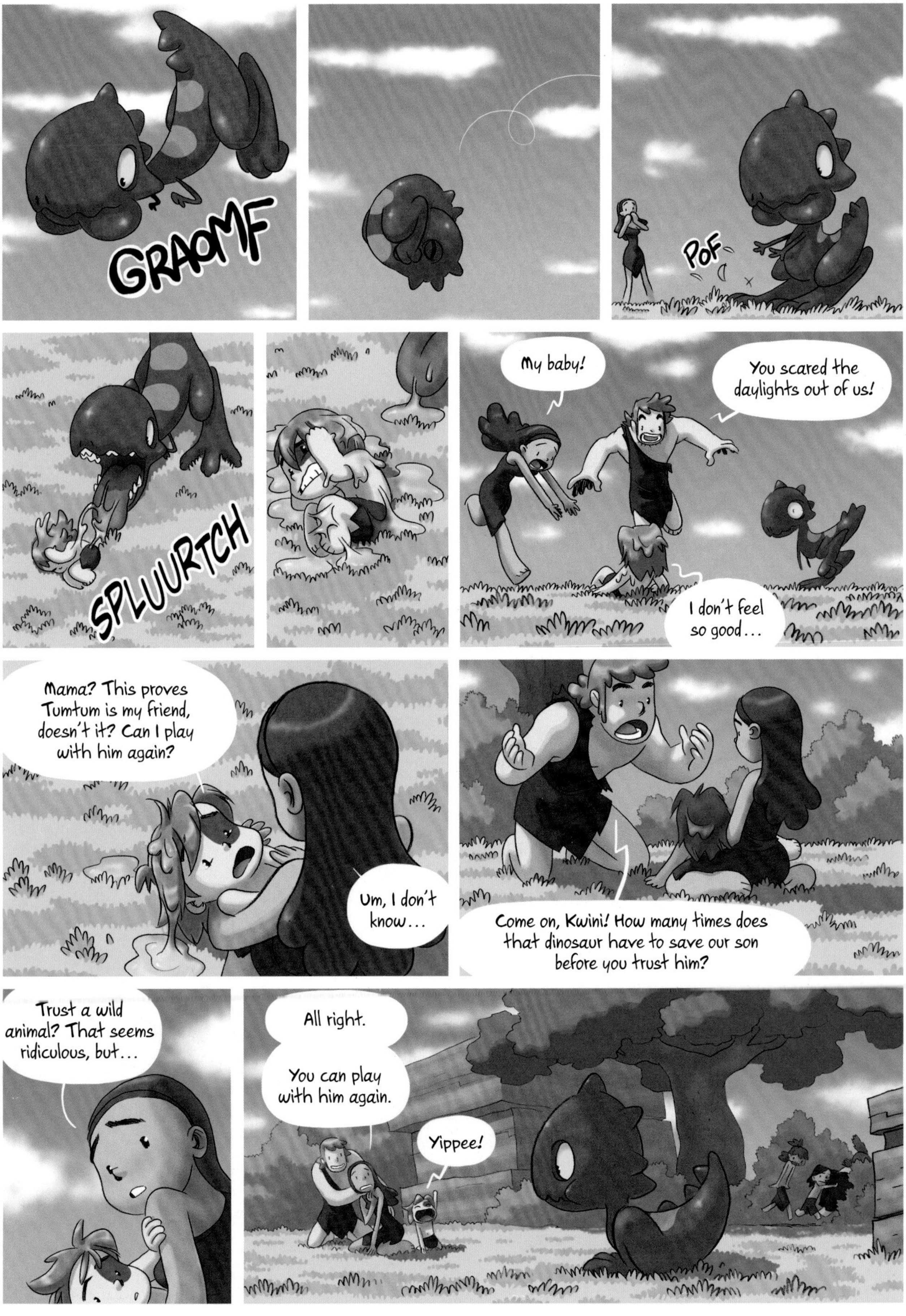
GRAOMF
POF
SPLUURTCH
My baby!
You scared the daylights out of us!
I don't feel so good...
Mama? This proves Tumtum is my friend, doesn't it? Can I play with him again?
Um, I don't know...
Come on, Kwini! How many times does that dinosaur have to save our son before you trust him?
Trust a wild animal? That seems ridiculous, but...
All right.
You can play with him again.
Yippee!

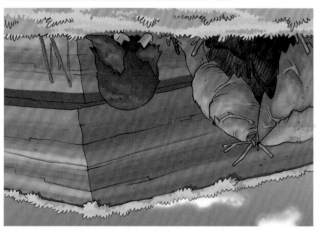

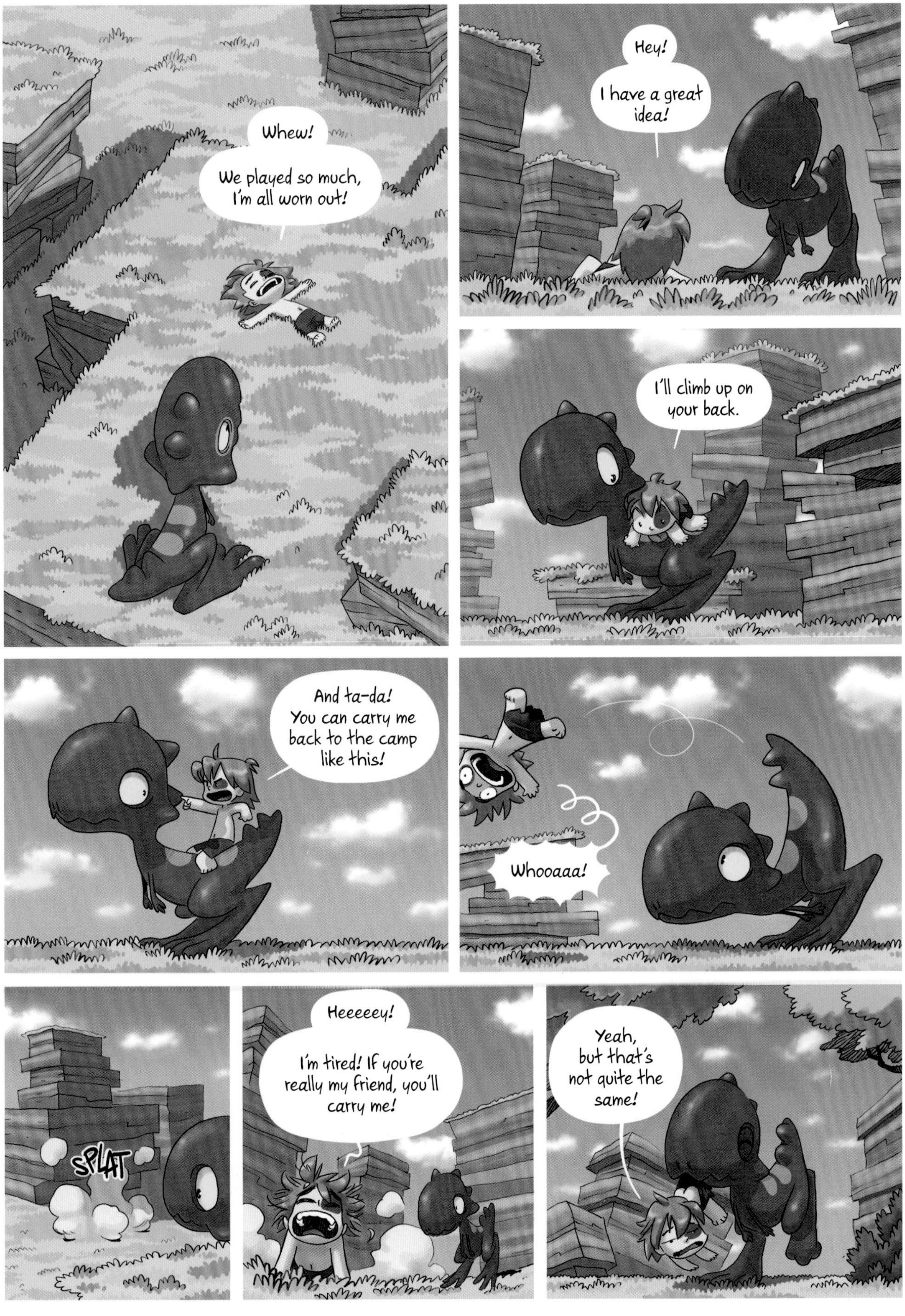
Whew!
We played so much, I'm all worn out!
Hey!
I have a great idea!
I'll climb up on your back.
And ta-da! You can carry me back to the camp like this!
Whooaaa!
SPLAT
Heeeeey!
I'm tired! If you're really my friend, you'll carry me!
Yeah, but that's not quite the same!

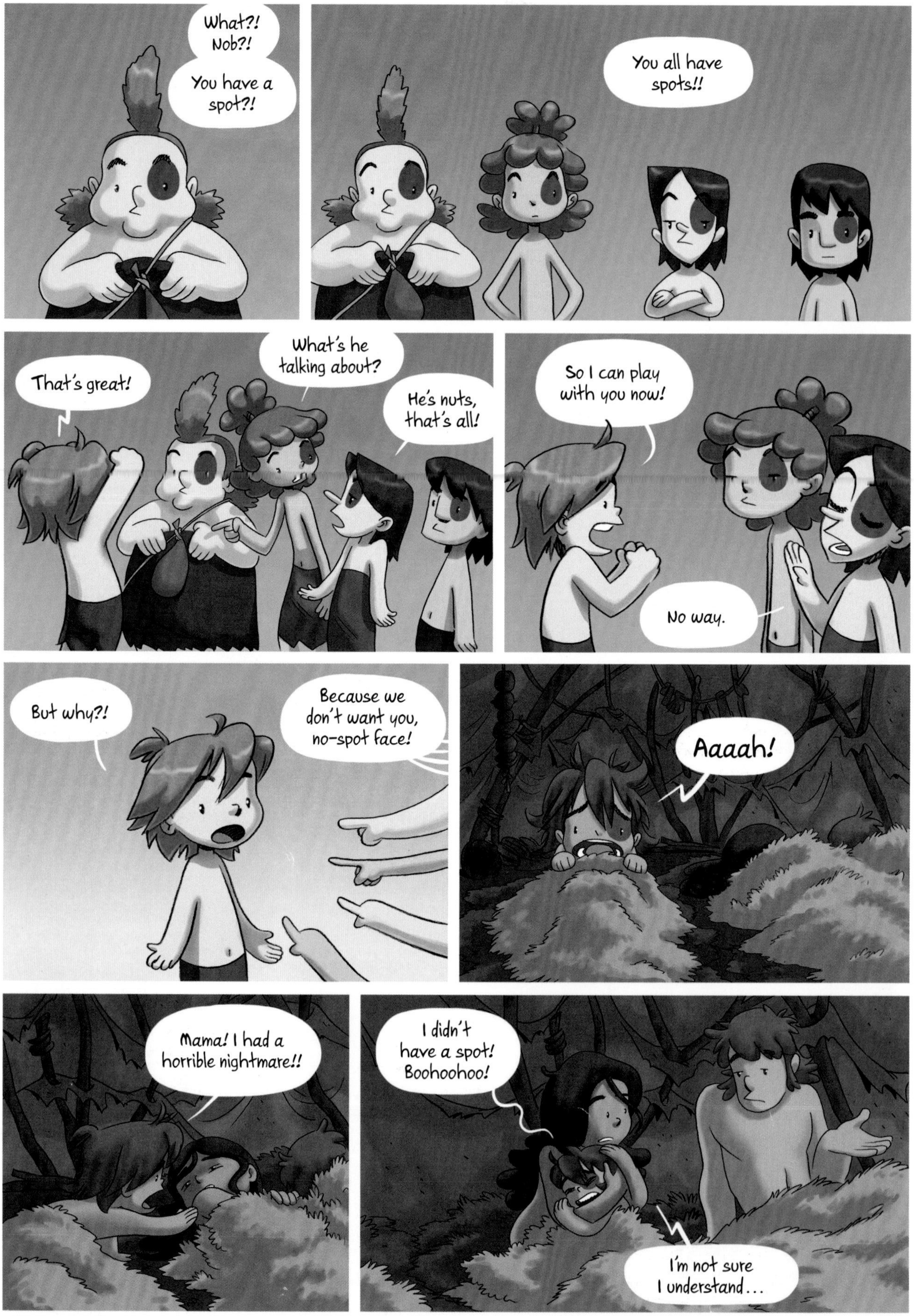
What?! Nob?!
You have a spot?!
You all have spots!!
That's great!
What's he talking about?
He's nuts, that's all!
So I can play with you now!
No way.
But why?!
Because we don't want you, no-spot face!
Aaaah!
Mama! I had a horrible nightmare!!
I didn't have a spot! Boohoohoo!
I'm not sure I understand...

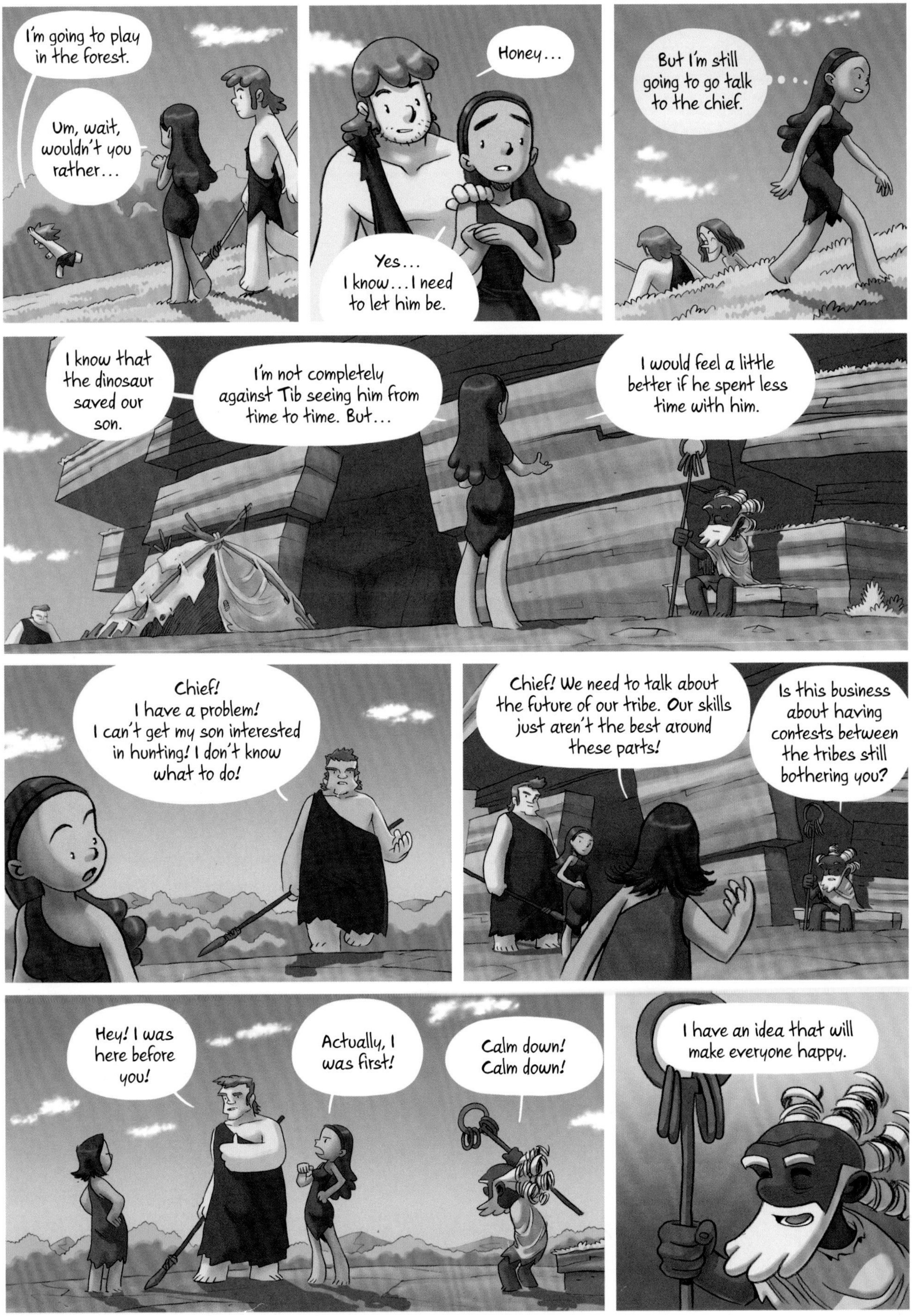
I'm going to play in the forest.
Um, wait, wouldn't you rather...
Honey...
Yes... I know... I need to let him be.
But I'm still going to go talk to the chief.
I know that the dinosaur saved our son.
I'm not completely against Tib seeing him from time to time. But...
I would feel a little better if he spent less time with him.
Chief! I have a problem! I can't get my son interested in hunting! I don't know what to do!
Chief! We need to talk about the future of our tribe. Our skills just aren't the best around these parts!
Is this business about having contests between the tribes still bothering you?
Hey! I was here before you!
Actually, I was first!
Calm down! Calm down!
I have an idea that will make everyone happy.

I can teach them how to use a spear!

Dressmaking!

Fishing!

Making fire!

Our parents look like they're having fun up there.

C'mon, are you gonna throw your rock?!

Who cares? It's nothing to do with us!

It's simple. Who is the best at tracking animals?

My husband, obviously!

Right, so it will be you, Lar, who teaches that skill to the children.

I've decided to start a Life Skills School!

Listen to me, everybody!

I don't get it.

Me neither.

How will that work?

It's time to try to improve how we pass on our knowledge.

Up until now, each person taught what he knew to his own children. From now on, we're going to group the children according to their age, and each adult will teach them whatever job they know how to do best.

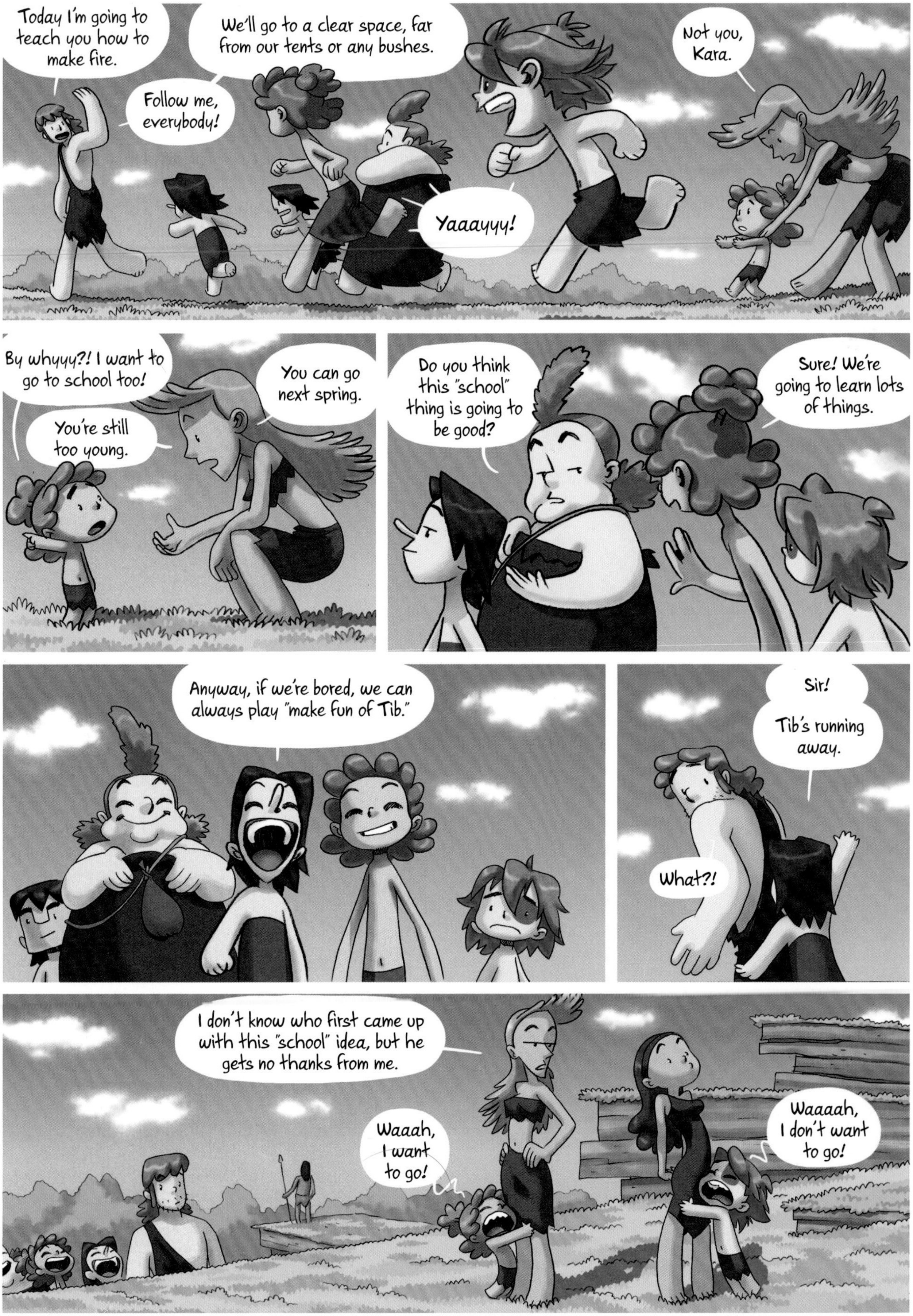
Today I'm going to teach you how to make fire.
Follow me, everybody!
We'll go to a clear space, far from our tents or any bushes.
Yaaayyy!
Not you, Kara.
By whyyy?! I want to go to school too!
You can go next spring.
You're still too young.
Do you think this "school" thing is going to be good?
Sure! We're going to learn lots of things.
Anyway, if we're bored, we can always play "make fun of Tib."
Sir!
Tib's running away.
What?!
I don't know who first came up with this "school" idea, but he gets no thanks from me.
Waaah, I want to go!
Waaaah, I don't want to go!

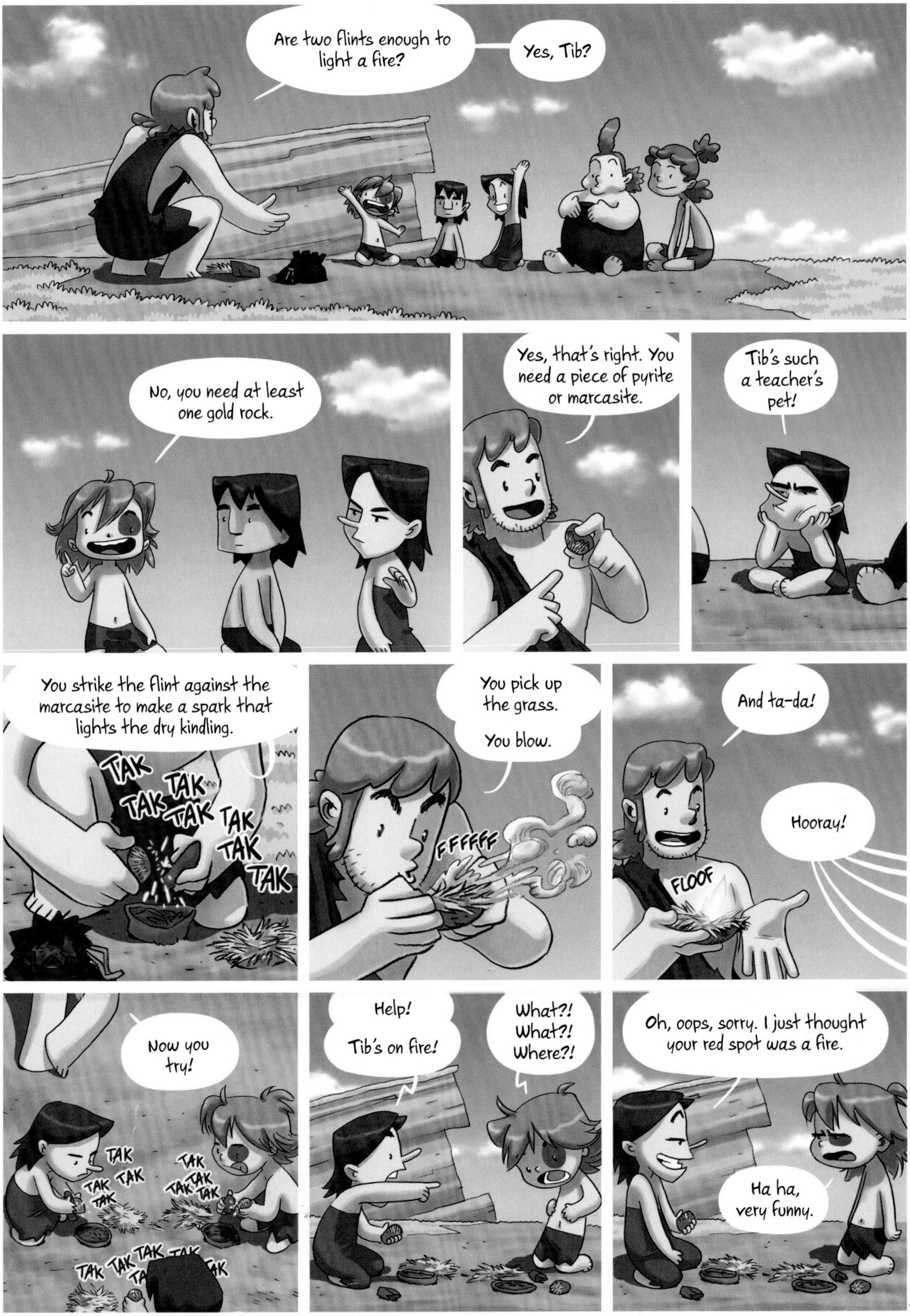
Are two flints enough to light a fire?
Yes, Tib?
No, you need at least one gold rock.
Yes, that's right. You need a piece of pyrite or marcasite.
Tib's such a teacher's pet!
You strike the flint against the marcasite to make a spark that lights the dry kindling.
TAK TAK TAK TAK TAK TAK TAK
You pick up the grass.
You blow.
FFFFFF
And ta-da!
FLOOF
Hooray!
Now you try!
TAK TAK TAK TAK
TAK TAK TAK TAK
Help!
Tib's on fire!
What?! What?! Where?!
Oh, oops, sorry. I just thought your red spot was a fire.
Ha ha, very funny.

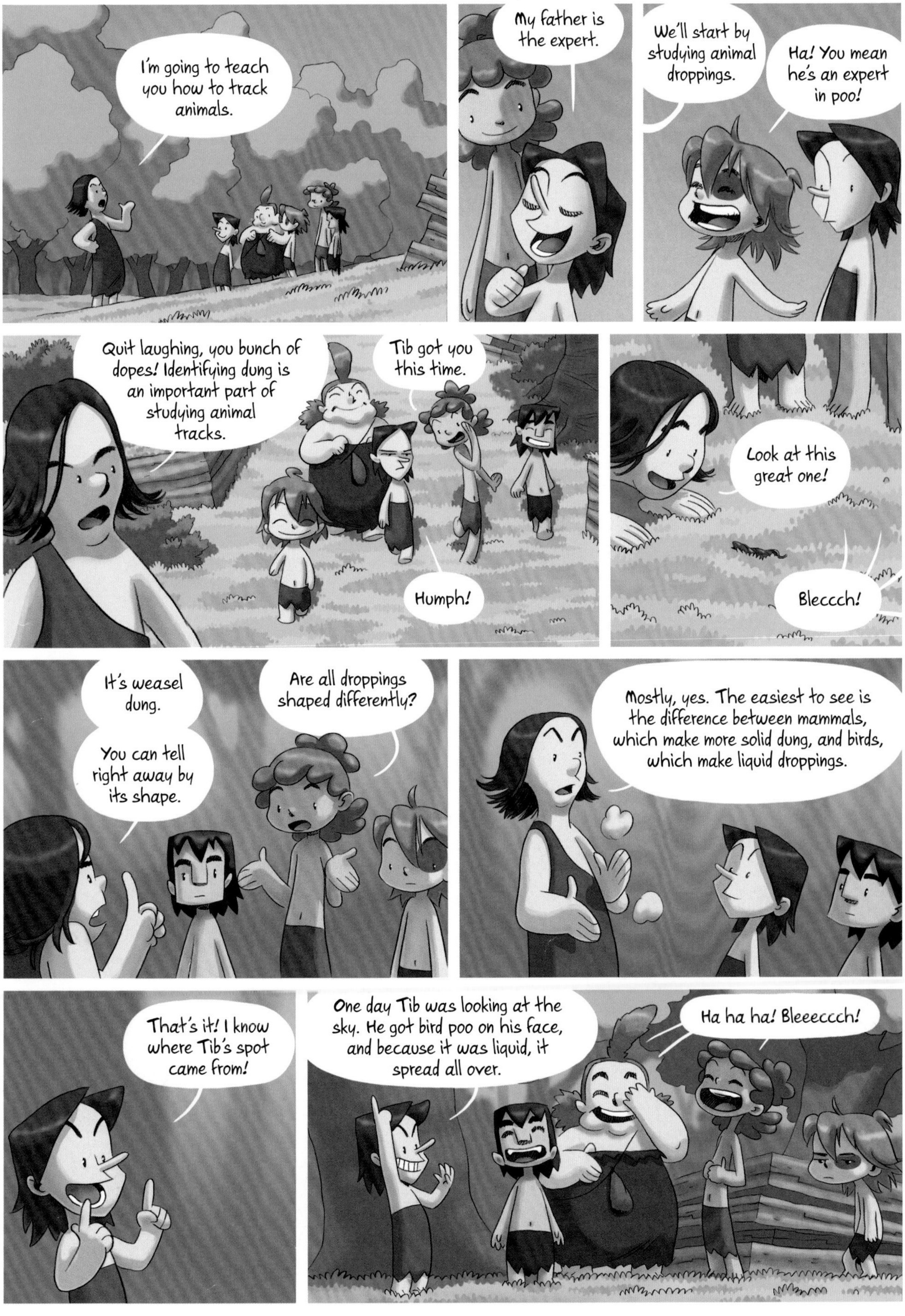
I'm going to teach you how to track animals.
My father is the expert.
We'll start by studying animal droppings.
Ha! You mean he's an expert in poo!
Quit laughing, you bunch of dopes! Identifying dung is an important part of studying animal tracks.
Tib got you this time.
Humph!
Look at this great one!
Bleccch!
It's weasel dung.
You can tell right away by its shape.
Are all droppings shaped differently?
Mostly, yes. The easiest to see is the difference between mammals, which make more solid dung, and birds, which make liquid droppings.
That's it! I know where Tib's spot came from!
One day Tib was looking at the sky. He got bird poo on his face, and because it was liquid, it spread all over.
Ha ha ha! Bleeeccch!

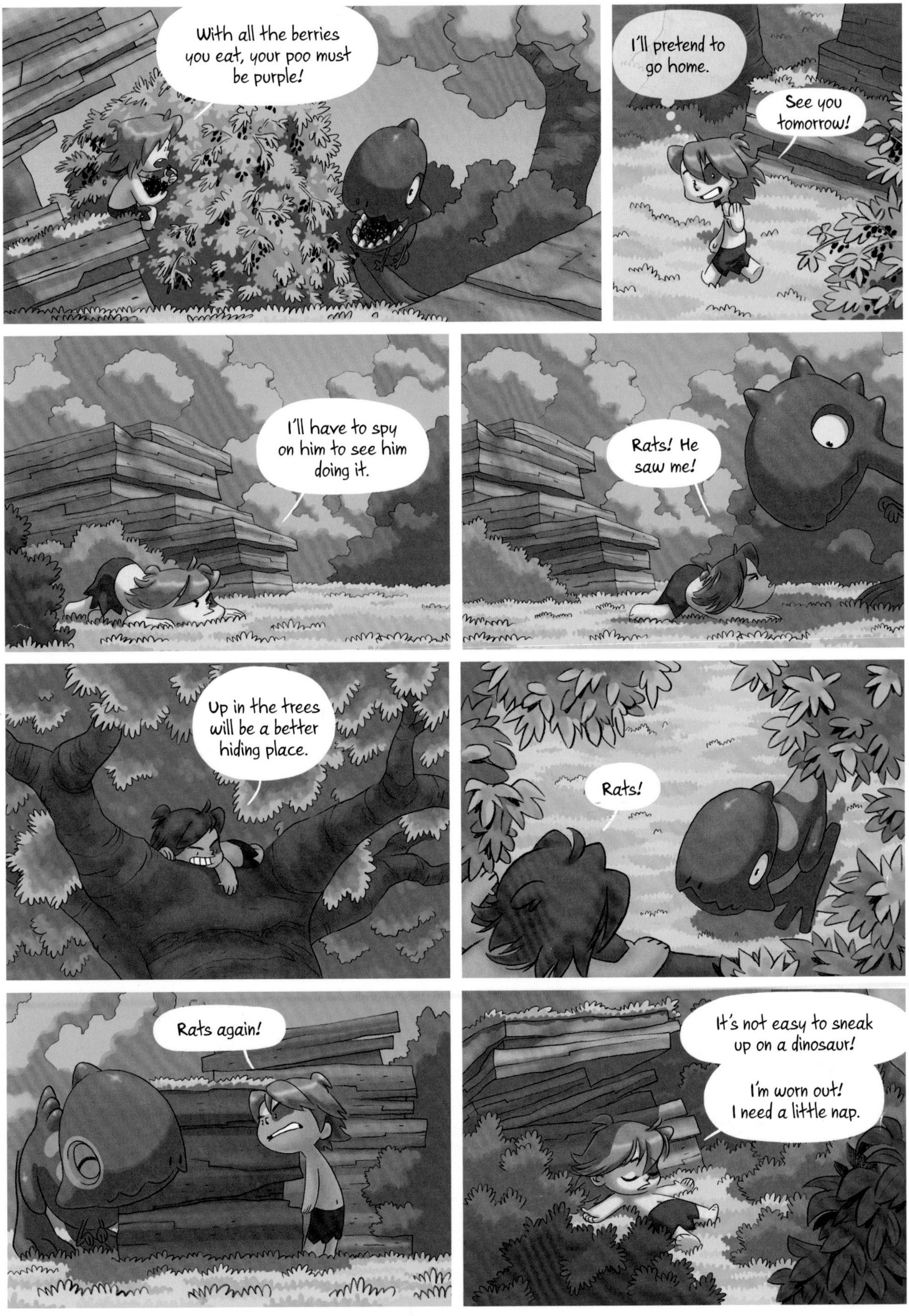
With all the berries you eat, your poo must be purple!
I'll pretend to go home.
See you tomorrow!
I'll have to spy on him to see him doing it.
Rats! He saw me!
Up in the trees will be a better hiding place.
Rats!
Rats again!
It's not easy to sneak up on a dinosaur!
I'm worn out! I need a little nap.

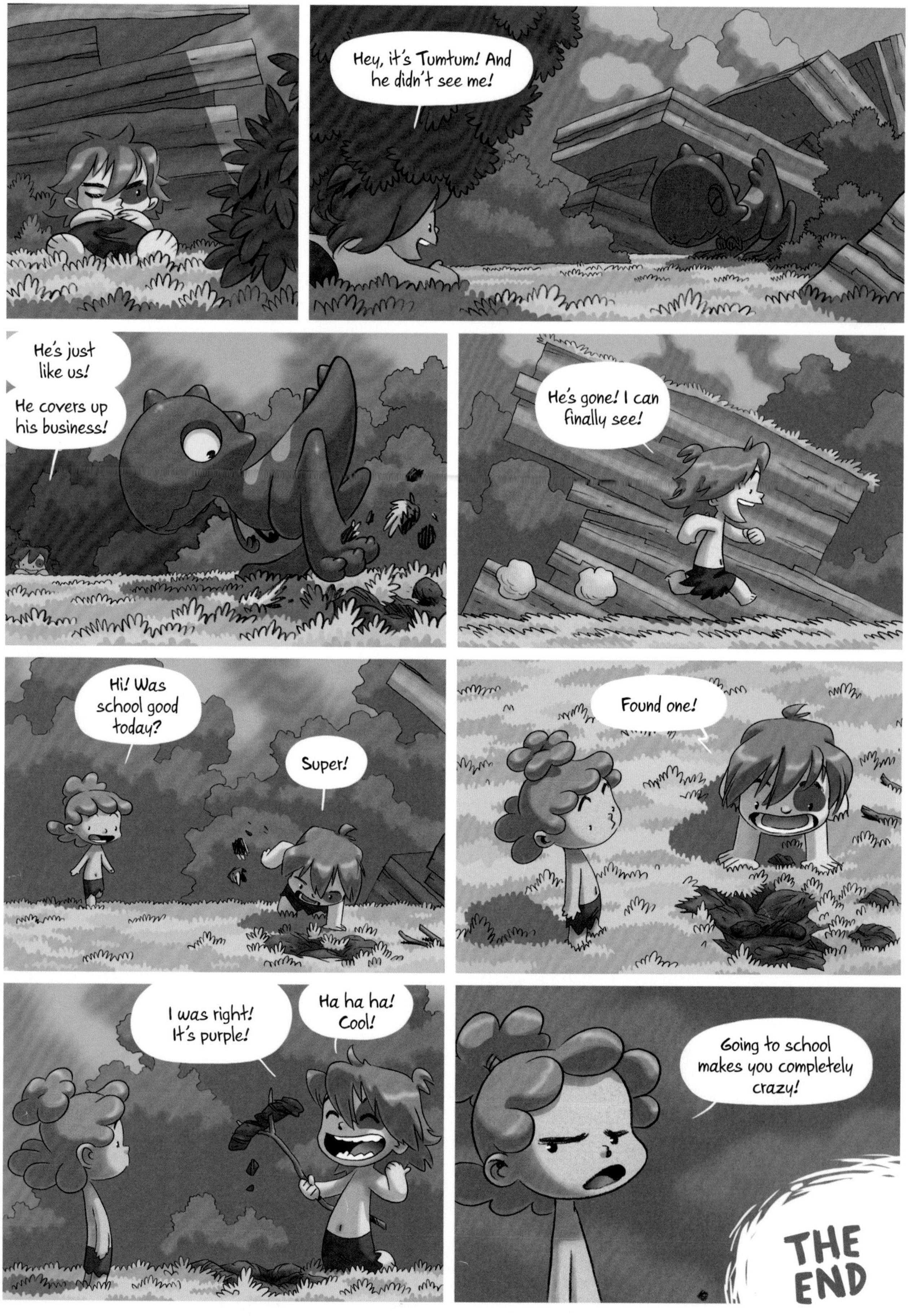
Hey, it's Tumtum! And he didn't see me!
He's just like us!
He covers up his business!
He's gone! I can finally see!
Hi! Was school good today?
Super!
Found one!
I was right! It's purple!
Ha ha ha! Cool!
Going to school makes you completely crazy!
THE END

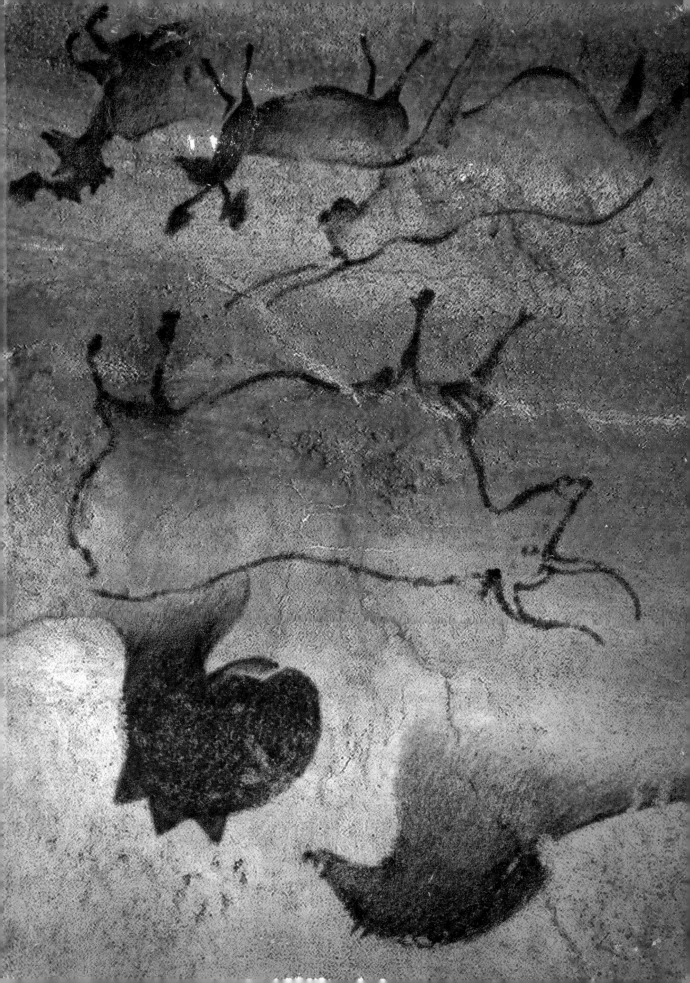